The Bo

C H Clepitt

The Book of Abisan.

Published using Lulu.com 2013

ISBN: 978-1-291-44290-8

For more information on the author visit www.chclepitt.com

Visit The Book of Abisan online at www.chclepitt.com/thebookofabisan

Part One: Inceptivus

Chapter One

Yfrey, the witch was tired. She looked up towards the sky. It was night. The crushing darkness was unmistakeable. For what seemed like an eternity, both the sun and the moons had been permanently enveloped by oppressive, angry rain clouds. When the sky was black, it was night. Day was signalled by the lighter shade of grey. She could not remember when exactly the rain had started; but it showed no sign of abating. Her life before she had been forced into exile was so long ago that it was as though it had happened to someone else. She felt she had been running forever.

The inquisition had lasted ten years, and still it showed no signs of coming to an end. Calim had preyed on the fears of government. He had warned that the women involved in the emancipation movement were dangerous, not just politically, but magically. Yfrey had seen many people taken for interrogation who never returned. Those who had been deemed guilty of exploring the dark arts had then been made an example of: burned alive or hung up-side-down from trees, guarded to prevent any attempt at rescue. If anyone was truly in league with the Devil it was Calim. People were too afraid to speak out against him. They turned on neighbours and friends in order to save their own skins. The irony was, that anyone truly capable of witchcraft, like Yfrey, had used their powers to escape, so it was mainly the innocent who were caught.

Yfrey came from the old order: a group of sorcerers so ancient that their magics were connected to the earth itself. When the inquisition first began, she and her brother, Torius, had fled to the woods, taking the historical volumes and the Book of Abisan with them. They had been confident that the trees and the earth would hide them from the soldiers. However, Torius had been militant. He had insisted on striking back, setting up calculated attacks on groups of soldiers, taking them out. He rescued several victims from trees, convincing them to join his quest. Becoming a folk hero, he had provided hope for the people. One day, however, he did not return from a raid. A week later Yfrey had heard soldiers approaching the camp where those left behind had been hiding. She had taken the Book of Abisan and fled. To increase their chances of survival the group had separated, and Yfrey had been alone for nearly a year now. She had kept moving as best she could; staying in the shadows and avoiding people as much as possible, as they were not to be trusted.

She was not just fleeing, however. The Book of Abisan contained prophecies about forthcoming events. It had predicted the inquisition. Her parents had tried to warn people; they were among the first to be convicted of witchcraft. Yfrey had translated a section of the book that offered hope. It spoke of a warrior, a Roghnaithe: a woman who would purge the land of evil, and free the Earth's true people. It stated that she would not know her true power, but would be taught, and protected by the Conduit: a powerful witch who would guide the Roghnaithe to her destiny.

Yfrey had decided that she must find the Conduit and help them in any way she could. She was not by any means a powerful witch, but she was able to channel the earth and elements and more importantly, she was able to read the Book of Abisan, which would be a critical tool in fighting this war. For the past three months she had been on the trail of Wrance, an elder in her parents' coven. She felt certain he would help her find the conduit. When the inquisition had begun, those not captured had all fled in different directions. Tracking anyone was problematic, if they left much of a trail they would not live long. However, Wrance drew his power from the earth. He was what was known as a Harvester. His magics ensured a fruitful harvest each year. His powers could not be channelled into anything more dangerous than stopping crops from reaching their full potential. The hunters were indiscriminate.

Yfrey had been communicating with the forest plants, and they had been mapping her way to Wrance. His trail had ended at the bottom of the cliff upon which she was now sitting. She had long given up seeking shelter from the rain. She had learned to embrace it. She had a bigger problem now. Wrance's trail had ended, which could mean one of two things: he was captured or dead. She was working under the assumption that he was captured. This presented her with the difficulty that he was going to be guarded by at least two men; getting to him would not be easy. She sighed, wrapped The Book of Abisan back up in its protective canvas, replaced it in her pack and silently began to make her way down the cliff. She ensured that she remained as close to the trees as possible, using her powers to make certain she was virtually invisible against them. When she reached the bottom of the cliff she could see through the darkness two guards standing in front of a large oak tree. Hanging from the tree was Wrance. His breathing was laboured, but she was unable to see his physical condition from her position behind some bushes. The guards were moaning loudly about the weather and being forced to stand out in the rain. Yfrey took a deep breath. If she was going to rescue Wrance she would need help. She raised her arms above her head and silently called upon the winds to help her. A strong wind blew through the trees, removing the guards' hats from their heads and extinguishing their torches. Yfrey then directed hail stones to bombard the guards as they fumbled around in the darkness for their hats.

"Aw, forget this!" one of them exploded. "No-one's gonna be stupid enough to try and rescue that sad old bag of bones in this! I'm outta here!"

"Hey!" the other called after his comrade as he retreated.

"Why won't you just leave?" Yfrey muttered to herself in frustration. She directed a lightning bolt directly at his feet.

"Argh!" he jumped out of the way. "Wait for me!"

When Yfrey was certain that the coast was clear, she moved in to free Wrance.

"Wrance! It's me, Yfrey," she hissed. "Don't worry; I'm going to get you out of here." She took her knife from her pack and began to saw at the ropes which held him.

"Yfrey! Thank the moons my prayers have been answered." As the rope finally gave way, she lowered him to the ground. "I knew you'd come," his breathing continued to be laboured. "I have so much to tell you, and there is so little time."

“Tell me later,” she hissed urgently. “We’ve got to get out of here now, there’s no telling how long those guards will stay away.”

“I can’t. My legs are broken. My journey ends here. It is you who must go on Yfrey.”

“No! I need your help to find The Conduit. I’ll get you to a safe place where you can heal.”

“Yfrey… you are the Conduit…”

“What? No! I can’t be! I don’t have nearly that kind of power.”

“It is written that The Conduit will find her power through hatred, which she must transform into love if she is to guide the Roghnaithe on the correct path.”

“Where is it written? And where does it say it’s me? I have studied The Book of Abisan, nowhere does it say it’s me! Come on, we’ve got to move.”

Just then a shot rang out. Wrance was no longer sitting up against the tree, but slumped down, bleeding from the chest. Yfrey froze for a moment. The guards advanced slowly, rifles pointing directly towards her.

“Give it up Girly, unless you want to end up like your friend,” one spoke, mockingly. “You’re a bit bedraggled, but the boys get lonely. It’ll be better than hanging by your toes.”

Yfrey slowly rose to her feet. She looked at the guards. They were not people. They were not even animals. Animals kill for food. These beings received some sort of sadistic pleasure from inflicting torture.

“Stay away from me,” her voice was low but clear. As she spoke, storm clouds rolled above her head.

“Ha! What you gonna do? Hide behind your pet corpse?” the guards continued to advance.

“I said stay away!” Yfrey raised her arms and called upon the elements to protect her. Two lightning bolts struck the guards. They did not even scream. They just fell to the ground, dead. Yfrey approached the charred corpses. She looked into the hideously deformed faces and felt nothing. She took the rifle and the ammunition from the bodies and hurried back to Wrance. His breathing was shallow.

“Wrance…” she spoke desperately. “I don’t know what to do.”

“You… are… the… Conduit…” the old man gasped. “When… the… rain… stops… your… path… will… become… clear…” with a final breath he was gone.

“Oh, Wrance.” Yfrey closed his eyes, gathered her things and started to move silently into the forest. There was no time for funeral rites. She had to keep moving. Conduit or not, one thing was clear, she was on her own. The rain showed no sign of stopping, so for now at least, she was blind.

Chapter Two

Jacques worked in the archives section of the city museum. She was based in the basement, below where the people generally congregated. There were no windows and the electric lighting made everything appear pale and withered. The job suited her, because very few people were interested in local or ancient history and thus required limited human interaction. The fewer people she had to deal with the happier she was. As a general rule she thought people shallow and uninteresting. It was not that she lacked social skills. Indeed, should the occasion call for it she could be very charming. It was more that she resented the falseness that accompanied pleasantries. Indeed, if it were not for her brother forcing his presence upon her once a week for dinner then she would shun contact with the outside world entirely. She had discovered in her teens that the best way to avoid human interaction was to appear as frightening as possible. She dyed her hair, which was naturally a mousy brown colour, jet black. She wore white face makeup with black lipstick and eye liner. Her nails were always painted either black or dark blue and she had a tattoo of a spider's web, which started at the nape of her neck and went halfway down her back. This image ensured that she was able to go through life generally uninterrupted by people and their minor concerns.

Sitting at a desk updating records before inputting them on the new electronic system, she heard a loud bang from the very back of the basement, accompanied by all the lights being extinguished. It was an old building and the basement had only recently been rewired to have electric lighting. Being a council run building, it had of course, been done on the cheap and this was the third time in as many weeks that the circuit had overloaded and blown the lights. She was supposed to call maintenance when this happened; they would send a man down to fix it. The last few times, however, it had taken him almost forty-five minutes to arrive. When he did arrive he had attempted to make friendly conversation with her rather than work quickly, which was just too irritating for words. She turned the torch function on her mobile phone on and headed towards the circuit breaker at the back of the room. Last time, all that had been necessary to rectify the situation was pulling a lever down and then pushing it up again. She felt she could handle that alone.

When she reached the fuse box she held her phone up close to it, to see if she could identify the problem. There was no problem. It was turned off. She had a sinking feeling in the pit of her stomach. There was a creaking sound behind her and a voice so twisted with hate that it was impossible to ascertain its gender. It screamed.

"Die! You Abomination!"

The creak had forewarned Jacques, however, and she instinctively ducked as something was swung at her head. Whatever it was smashed into the circuit breaker with a crash. There was a great flood of light, followed by an agonising howl of pain and the smell of charred flesh. There was a thud. Jacques rose to her feet and carefully moved towards the body, which was still smoking. She lit the face. It was contorted in pain, but seemed to be male. She did not recognise him. She hurried up the stairs and out of the basement to call the police, as she had no signal where she was.

The questions went on for hours. Was she sure that she did not know the man who had attacked her? Who would want to hurt her? Had she seen anything suspicious prior to today? She could not answer any of them. After what seemed like an eternity she heard a voice she recognised.

"Excuse me, Officer, I'm looking for my sister."

"Ben?"

"Jacques! What happened?"

"I told them not to call you, I'm fine."

"You aren't fine. Someone tried to kill you. Do we know who he was?"

"We have been unable to identify the perpetrator at this time, Father. He had no identification on him, and the high voltage has made visual identification problematic." The police officer addressed Ben with the respect afforded a man of the cloth.

"He attacked me with some sort of weird knife, hit the fuse box instead! Lucky he wasn't a cricket fan I guess."

"Very. Can I take her home now please? I think she's been through enough for one day."

"Sure. If you think of anything then don't hesitate to call."

"I will."

"I've brought my car, I'll drive you home."

As he spoke Ben tried to put a comforting arm around his sister's shoulder, but she brushed him off.

"I told you, I'm fine. You didn't need to come."

"Of course I came. You're my sister."

"Isn't everybody your brother or sister? Isn't that what that stupid collar means?"

"Jacques, I don't want to get into this with you now. And you aren't driving me away. I'm making sure you get home safely whether you like it or not."

"Fine. I can handle myself though, you know that."

"I know, it's just for my own peace of mind."

"Just so we're clear."

"We are."

"Good. It's not like you'd be much use in a fight anyway, what with your 'turn the other cheek' crap."

"Well, I have friends in high places."

"Whatever."

* * *

Her flat was the vacant space above a garage. There were metal steps leading up the outside of the building for access separate from the workspace below. As they pulled up outside Ben turned off the engine and unbuckled his seatbelt.

"You aren't going to walk me in?"

"Well, I fancied a cup of that herbal crap you drink."

"Hey! My body is a temple."

Ben raised his eyebrows and looked at her tattoos, but knew better than to enter into that conversation.

"Come on then," she said as she exited the car. "Kettle won't boil itself."

Jacques was up the steps and through the door before Ben had even locked the car. She left the door open for him as she went in to boil the kettle. Clearly the church frowned upon exercise as pastime, and all that communion wine had given him quite a notable beer belly.

"Someone... left... this... outside..." he panted, as he eventually made it into the kitchen to join her.

It was an oddly shaped package, wrapped in brown paper and tied with string. He placed it on the coffee table and collapsed in a chair, the exertion of stair climbing proving entirely too much for him.

"Man, you need to do some exercise," as she spoke she put the mugs down on the table. "Just cos you've given up sex, that's no excuse to let yourself go."

She picked up the package and examined it, turning it around in her hands trying to find some clue as to what was inside.

"I haven't ordered anything."

"Why don't you open it?" Ben suggested, taking a sip of the yellowish green liquid with which he had been presented.

She seated herself opposite him and began to unpick the knots in the string. After what seemed like an eternity she released the bonds and the paper fell away. On her lap was something wrapped in oil cloth. Ben leaned in towards her with fascination, to get a closer look. She delicately lifted away the cloth to reveal a dagger in a sheath.

"Wow."

She lifted it on the palms of both hands in order to examine it more closely. It smelt like old leather and metal and as she pulled the sheath away slightly a coppery odour of blood mixed itself with the other smells. The hilt was ornate, engraved with characters that she did not recognise and there was a jewel in the middle, which glistened different colours in the light.

"Wow," she said again.

"Who would send you such a thing?" Ben was unable to take his eyes off the blade.

"Someone who knows me really well."

She had now unsheathed the knife and was getting a feel for the weight of it in her hands.

"I don't like it."

"You don't like anything! It's kinda your job to disapprove," the insult was half hearted as she was more interested in motioning with the knife, making slow motion combative moves. "Don't worry, I'll keep it in my floor safe."

She sheathed the blade, put it down on the table and picked up her drink.

"So, you want me to make up the sofa for you or will the nuns worry?"

Chapter Three

Yfrey had not had time to process the information that Wrance had given her. She had not stopped moving all night. She felt no remorse for what had happened to the guards. She felt nothing. Despite the years of hardship, she had endured her survival instinct was still strong and it told her to keep going – to get as far away from the scene of the crime as possible. The blinding darkness and rain had made navigating the woods difficult, and now that the grey light of dawn was upon her and visibility had improved she could see a clearing ahead. It was inevitable that in order to move continuously one would come upon clearings and populated areas. The trick was, when these things happened, to blend in. Being drenched to the bone and stained with Wrance's blood, Yfrey had little chance of blending into anything other than a war-zone. She stopped uncertainly. A part of her wanted to double back, but she knew where she had come from and that way lay no good. At the edge of the clearing was a small cottage. There was a well to the left of it and a chopping block just outside the front door. A small, makeshift shelter a little way ahead seemed to house chickens, and a bedraggled looking cockerel sat atop it, clearly too depressed to crow. It was still early. If she moved quickly she could be on the other side and protected once more by the cover of the forest. She decided to hurry.

In her haste to be invisible once more Yfrey did not notice the low fence of barbed wire that framed the cottage and its surrounding area. The wire was not hidden, and was so low that it could easily be stepped over. It was most likely designed to serve as a deterrent to the chickens escaping, than any sort of defence against intruders. Yfrey, however, was utterly exhausted. She rarely slept and the perpetual battering of rain against her body was exhausting. Something had to give, and in this instance it was her footing. She flew head first over the wire and landed with an unceremonious thud in the mud of the clearing. The sudden noise of her expedient contact with the ground startled the chickens which began to squawk and cackle incessantly. She tried to get up quickly and keep moving but her ankle was still attached to the wire and bleeding profusely. She could not move. The mud was too slippery to right herself and every time she tried to twist her ankle free of the wire its grip became more determined.

The mixture of pain, blood loss and exhaustion started to make the world around her blur. The sound of the chickens dulled into the background until all she could hear was the wind. She was barely aware of the old man who emerged from the cottage, untangled her ankle and dragged her through the mud and inside. She was semi-conscious as he undressed her, cleaned the mud from her body and wrapped her in clean clothes. She watched as he cleaned her wounded ankle, put some strange green inside the deep cuts and bandaged it tightly. She knew it was happening, but was unable to move or react. Had this man wanted to kill her he could have done so easily. When he had finished tending her injuries he ladled some odd looking broth from a cauldron over the fire and held it up to her lips.

"Drink this," he said quietly. "It will help you to heal and sleep. You look like you haven't slept in an eternity."

Yfrey could not actually remember the last time she had slept. She was not in any physical condition to refuse the odd tasting broth. It had a woody, peppery taste, and coated her tongue and throat like thick mud. She barely managed two mouthfuls before passing out.

When she came to she was alone, in a warm bed, with a glass of water and a walking cane next to her. She looked around drowsily. There had obviously been some sort of sleeping drug in the broth. She had not slept properly for years. Constantly aware of the dangers that surrounded her, she was always prepared to run at the slightest sense of danger, and as such her sleeping had been shallow and hyper aware. She had not even noticed being moved to the bed. The luxury of waking up slowly in a warm bed was one that she had scarce been afforded. She tried to fight the drowsy feeling that now engulfed her. She had to keep moving. Her ankle could not take her weight and she fell back heavily onto the bed. She reached across to the walking cane and used it to support her movements. Cautiously she opened the bedroom door. Before her was a corridor. It led to a large window at one end, looking out onto the forest. There were three closed doors leading to she knew not where, and one open door at the very end. Her movement was impeded by the pain in her ankle and running was not an option. She had two choices. She could stay in the room and wait to see what was going to happen, or she could go through the end door and find out now. She had never been very good at waiting. She moved slowly and painstakingly towards the door, relying heavily on the cane.

The old man was stirring a pot over the stove. Upon hearing her enter, he stopped what he was doing and turned to face her.

"Well, hello there," he spoke in a friendly tone to which Yfrey was unaccustomed. "You must have a strong constitution. The dose I gave you should have knocked you out for a week. It's only been three days."

"Three days?" Yfrey repeated slowly.

"Yes, it was a healing poultice. By the time you woke up you should have been fully healed. Never mind, take a seat, your ankle must hurt. I'm making chicken stew."

Yfrey glanced out of the window at the chickens. Their numbers sadly depleted. She hated the custom of killing animals to eat them. It seemed so unnecessary when the Earth was so generous.

"You're a healer?" she asked after a moment.

"Yes. And you're a witch. No-one else could have fought off my poultice so quickly. Don't worry, you're safe here."

He opened his shirt slightly to reveal the brand of the witch hunters: a huge cross burnt into his chest.

"Do you have powers?"

"No, but my method of healing, using herbs rather than surgery is too effective to be natural. No-one comes here, and I go no-where. You're quite safe. Do you have powers?"

"I'm a harvester," she lied. "But with all the rain it's been difficult."

"Maybe you can help my herb garden grow whilst you're here."

“I have to keep moving. The longer I stay here the more danger I put you in.”

“I told you, no-one comes here. You shouldn’t leave until you’re healed. You won’t be going anywhere very fast on that ankle. Besides, I’d enjoy the company.”

“Well... alright,” she said hesitantly. “I’m Yfrey.”

“Portan.”

The old man smiled and handed her a bowl of stew.

They ate in companionable silence. In a world where neighbour turned on neighbour, one learnt quickly that the key to survival was not to ask too many questions. Yfrey had a price on her head because of her militant brother, and she suspected that Portan did not live alone in the middle of a forest through preference. When they had finished eating Portan stood up and took her bowl.

“If you can bring yourself to stay another three days,” he said, “the poultice I put on your wound will continue to heal you. You should be able to move normally.”

“I fear that I would put you in terrible danger by remaining in your home.” Yfrey began. In truth she could not think of anywhere she would rather be. She could not remember how long it had been since she had enjoyed the comfort of shelter and a bed to sleep in. She would never stay in one place too long.

“No-one comes here,” Portan assured her. “Since The Inquisition people would rather go to the bleeders, or just die quietly rather than risk being associated with someone like me. You’re quite safe here. No-one has visited me in years.”

“Alright then, but only until my foot is healed.”

Chapter Four

Jacques' work colleagues were trying to be extra sensitive towards her since "the incident". Whereas usually they would leave her alone to do her job in peace, only communicating work related queries, which she was more than capable of addressing professionally and quickly. Now, they were attempting to make small talk. This, she was less equipped to deal with. People were gently touching her arm as they spoke to her and perpetually asking "how are you doing?" Usually her curt, short replies served as a deterrent to such attempts at conversation. However, now people seemed to be making allowances for her manner, due to her recent trauma and her bluntness just caused them to make more of an effort. It was utterly infuriating. She could not get half an hour's work done without someone popping down to the basement with a cup of tea or a sandwich.

She had totally given up any hope of getting any work done for at least a month. Having just finished archiving an Egyptian urn which, when working at her usual pace would have been done hours ago her concentration was interrupted by the door creaking open again. She rolled her eyes in total exasperation. If it was Margery with another cup of tea and digestive biscuit she would not be responsible for her actions. She moved swiftly and silently down an aisle of WW2 artefacts and ducked down. If she could not find her, then hopefully Margery would take her tea and sympathy elsewhere and leave her in peace. Jacques was fully aware of how childish hiding from a co-worker was. She simply could not see any alternative. She was not naturally confident in confrontational situations; usually her appearance was enough to ensure that people avoided her.

The door creaked shut. Jacques listened intensely to determine whether Margery was going to make a more thorough sweep of the area before realising there was no-one there and retreating to the staff canteen. The heavy footsteps on the metal staircase told her it was not Margery. She felt an intense anxiety in the pit of her stomach as she crouched in her hiding place. As she watched the heavy, military style steel capped boots began to move around the basement she started to consider her options. Should she attempt to run, or find some sort of weapon and fight? She had trained in a number of martial arts, and knew enough to be quite formidable in a combat situation. She had not, however, been in a combat situation since achieving her third Dan almost five years ago, and did not particularly want to have to put her skills to the test. So she crouched, perfectly still, watching the large man move heavily around the basement, prodding at things. As he walked past the waste paper basket he gave it a hefty kick. Jacques estimated that he was far enough away from the staircase now for her to make a run for it and be at the top of the staircase before he noticed. She was about to make a bolt for it when the door creaked open again. She bit her lip in utter frustration, drawing blood. It tasted like copper in her mouth. Her heart was pounding so hard in her chest now she felt certain that were this giant man to stop crashing about and listen he would surely hear her. Then she heard a voice from halfway down the staircase that she recognised.

"Jacques? Are you here?"

"Ben! No! Don't!"

She rushed out from her hiding place with the automatic instinct to protect her hapless brother. He always arrived at the most inconvenient times. One thing was perfectly clear to her; she was far more equipped to defend him than he was to defend himself. The power of prayer would simply not be enough against this enormous adversary.

As she hastened to warn her brother the large man moved with surprising agility and grabbed her by the throat. She felt herself raised off the ground as though she weighed nothing. His hand was huge and rough, and he lifted her to his eye level, inspecting her critically. His face was massive and scarred, his hair long and wild and his eyes were black as night and filled with hatred. His entire countenance was terrifying. Jacques could not defend herself against this man. She was so petrified she could not move.

"Gotcha," he said as though he were speaking to a rat that had been plaguing his home for weeks and he had finally captured it. "I was expecting you to be more impressive," he snorted.

"Hey!" Ben had made his way to the bottom of the stairs. The exertion of the speed of movement was making him audibly wheeze and the idea of this giant man paying any attention to this ludicrous spectacle was ridiculous. The giant man moved Jacques out of his eye line in order to look directly at Ben.

"Put her down right now!" Ben wheezed.

"Yes, Sir." The man released his grip immediately, dropping her from a height of about two feet. She landed heavily and went over on one ankle. It was sprained and she could not stand. She pulled herself to a safe distance from her assailant.

"The police are on their way," Ben continued. "You will be arrested if you stay here."

"Yes, Sir."

He walked calmly past Ben and up the stairs towards the exit. There were shouts of "Police! Stop!" and some crashing from behind the door. Ben moved quickly to where Jacques was sitting on the floor shaking, he crouched down next to her.

"Are you alright?"

"What the hell do you think?"

"Sorry, silly question. Can you stand?"

"I don't know. I've hurt my ankle."

"Here." He offered her an arm for support and helped her to her feet.

"Did you know who he was?"

"No. The woman upstairs called me straight after they called the police. They were worried about you."

"But he called you Sir, and did what you said. Why would he do that?"

"I don't know."

"I just attract psychos don't I?"

"Must be your winning personality."

"Must be."

The police questioned her for hours this time. Did she know who the man was? Who would want to hurt her? She was still unable to answer. As the large man had had no trouble knocking over two policemen and making his escape the officers in attendance were unable to question him as to his motives. More frighteningly, it meant that he was still out there. For this reason the police recommended Jacques not return to work until the matter was resolved. The manager at the museum agreed that this was the safest thing and assured her that her job would be waiting for her when things had settled down. Ben drove her home. She needed his help to climb the stairs to the flat, and was too exhausted to argue when he insisted on coming in. He helped her to elevate her ankle on the arm of the sofa and put some ice on it before heading to the kitchen to make drinks.

"Some of that herbal stuff?" he called through, trying to sound casual, despite the crack in his voice.

"There's a bottle of vodka under the sink. I'll have that, you have what you want."

Ben brought her in the bottle and a glass without saying a word. He almost always had a disapproving comment when she drank spirits, but they were both severely shaken by the day's events.

"You gonna stay over?" Jacques demanded whilst pouring her second glass.

"Of course, if you want me to."

"Lock the door then."

Chapter Five

Yfrey stayed with Portan for three weeks. The two had become accustomed to one another's company and a pleasant coexistence had developed between them. Yfrey showed the old man how to forage in the surrounding forest for mushrooms and berries, making his diet more varied and leaving the chickens free to lay eggs. She did not tell him anything about her past, and he did not ask. At night, when she was alone, she would study The Book of Abisan for clues as to where she would find The Conduit. It was very vague, as it was with most prophecies, but there were hints that a great magical battle was coming. As far as Yfrey was aware, magic had only ever been used as a tool for life. To help the harvest, or to heal wounds. She could see how it was possible for magic to be used in warfare – its purpose so bastardised that it could result in the destruction of the world. What was most disturbing to her was that in order for there to be a magical battle, those capable of magic would have to fight on the side of Callim. Yfrey could not imagine anyone who had been persecuted for so many years wanting to aid their persecutor. One thing was absolutely clear. The prophecy was there and it was her job to prevent it coming into fruition. She must find The Conduit, help guide them to the Roghnaithe and take Calim down before this apocalyptic scenario could occur. She had never felt more lost. Wrance was her last hope of finding The Conduit, and he was dead. The clues were vague. She refused to believe that she was The Conduit. Her powers were simply not strong enough. It was true that an intense surge of emotion seemed to strengthen her powers, but she relied heavily on the earth – her strength was not hers alone.

It was dusk. She was sitting on the bed in the small room, which over the course of three weeks had become hers. By the light of a small oil lamp she studied The Book of Abisan intensely. The same prophecy continued to trouble her. She drew a circle in the blankets with her finger to represent the earth. She drew a cross near the edge to represent herself and focused her mind on the image she had created. As the spell began to work, the image lifted itself and transformed from barely visible indentations in the bed linen to a full projection of the earth. Where she had marked herself glowed with tiny illumination. She cupped her hands so that the projected globe sat within them.

"Show me The Conduit," she commanded.

The glow of her location became more intense. Could it be true? Wrance was right? She had wasted her time looking for something which she already had? She did not feel ready, but she would become ready. She would train. She was in a reasonably secure location here. The earth was protecting her. She would use her time to prepare.

"Fine," she spoke at normal volume, although the spell did not require audible commands. "Then show me The Roghnaithe."

The projection of the earth began to spin violently. In shock, she pulled her hands away and it rose to eye level with her. The light that was her, blurred with the speed of movement. Then the image split. Suddenly there were two earths, two lights, each a reflection of the other, both spinning.

The sound of a crash from downstairs broke Yfrey's trance and ended the spell. Startled, she closed the book and hid it under her pillow. She moved swiftly and silently across the landing and to the top of the stairs. Staying below the banister so as not to draw attention to herself she peered through a knot hole to see what was going on. Two thugs from Calim's Royal Guard had kicked the door down and were standing over Portan, who had been knocked off his feet and was bleeding from the head.

"Now, we've 'ad reports that you bin 'arbouring a witch, Old Man," one said mockingly. "Tell us where she is an' we'll be on our way all peaceful like."

"Please," Portan spoke weakly. "There's no-one here but me. You can look around if you like, I've nothing to hide."

"Well, we could do that," the other thug spoke now. "But you see, witches is tricksy things. They can make themselves invisible and the like. Why don't you just tell us eh?" With this he kicked Portan in the guts.

Yfrey felt the black rage come over her that she had felt only once before in her life. It had not ended well for Calim's guards then and it certainly would not now. She stood up and walked slowly, calmly down the stairs.

"I think you're looking for me." She looked straight at the guards, undaunted by them.

"Blow me, we've got a stupid one here."

"I'll come quietly, just leave the old man be."

"Yfrey! No!" Portan looked helplessly at her.

"Shut it you," the guard gave another kick for effect. "Where's the fun if you come quietly?"

"Do you know who I am?" she asked calmly.

"I do." A new voice entered the cottage. Both guards fell to their knees in supplication at this new presence. He wore the black robes and white collar of a high priest/inquisitor in Calim's court. The jewelled cross around his neck spoke of his importance and authority.

"Yfrey," he spoke calmly. "I'm surprised you told the old man your real name. You were being so careful until now."

"So, you know who I am."

Yfrey was not intimidated by this man. She was struggling to hide the contempt in her voice. For her plan to work she had to get these three outside.

"Everyone knows who you are."

"Well those two idiots don't."

"To be fair, they are profoundly stupid."

"I can tell. Now that I'm speaking to the master and not the dogs will you accept my terms? I'll come with you willingly if you will guarantee Portan's safety."

"I believe you will come with us anyway."

"Is that a risk you want to take? Look at him – he's old and broken, not a threat to you."

"Yfrey..." Portan's tone was almost pleading.

"I'll be alright," Yfrey smiled weakly at the old man. "Promise."

"Don't make promises you can't keep. Shall we?" The Inquisitor stepped to one side, allowing Yfrey to leave in front of him. As he followed he looked down at the two prostrate guards and said, "Burn the place to the ground."

Once outside, Yfrey turned to face The Inquisitor, who had followed her out. He had taken a noose from his pocket, which he clearly expected her to wear on her journey to prison.

"You killed the chickens."

"Yes."

"You should not have done that."

"Why?"

"Because death feeds the earth." She closed her eyes and looked down for a moment. When she looked up the bodies of the chickens were gone, absorbed into the earth. The Inquisitor was buried up to his neck, staring at her helplessly.

"Call your men out of the cottage."

"What?"

"Do it now. This is not going to end well for you."

"Men! Come here!"

The two guards hurried out of the building.

"But we haven't set the fire yet..." one began. Then he stopped, clearly confused by the image that was before him.

"Stop now." Yfrey said calmly.

The two men stopped and looked at her.

"You killed the chickens." They stared at her blankly. "I liked the chickens." She raised her arms above her head and once more called upon the elements. There was a flash of lightning, followed by a crack of thunder, then, silence. The smoking corpses of the guards flanked the still visible head of the inquisitor.

"You killed my men."

"Yes."

"Are you going to kill me?"

"I think so."

“I’m a powerful man. I could be of use to you. I could speak to Calim, say you are not a threat, not worth our time.”

“He won’t believe you. I wasn’t a threat. I have become one through necessity. Now I am his worst nightmare, and I can’t allow you to live to report that back to him.”

“Yfrey! What did you do?” Portan had struggled to the entrance of the cottage with the assistance of the cane that only a few weeks ago had been Yfrey’s, and was surveying the carnage that surrounded him.

“I killed them.”

“Not all of them.”

“Not yet.”

“Old man! I can make you very rich if you help me. I have money, jewels. You can have immunity from prosecution. I’m important, my life has value.”

“You do not remember me.” Portan hobbled around until he was in front of The Inquisitor. “Perhaps we all look the same after a while. But I remember you. How could I ever forget?” He ripped open his shirt to reveal the cross that was branded onto his chest. “I will never forget you!” and with that he started to beat the head with his stick. Yfrey watched with fascination as the old man bludgeoned the head of The Inquisitor until it was unrecognisable as anything that was once living. Still she felt nothing. It seemed that the only emotions she was now capable of were all consuming hatred and rage. She knew that this was all that was keeping her alive and embraced it. Portan had stopped beating the corpse and collapsed in the mud. Tears were streaming down his cheeks.

“Did it help?”

“No, he’ll still be in my dreams every night, and I’ll still have a reminder of him burnt onto my chest. He’ll never be gone.”

Yfrey frowned. This was not something she was equipped to deal with. She would not know where to begin. She could not deal with people or emotions. She had no memory of what it was to experience either. She could, however, deal with the immediate problem.

"Go inside and clean yourself up, I'll deal with this." She closed her eyes and once more faced the earth. When she raised her head the evidence of the day's events had been swallowed.

How the men had arrived at the cottage was unclear. Presumably they had left their vehicles on the outskirts of the forest and attempted to navigate the trees on foot. No-one had reported them. No-one had been out this far into the forest. This meant that Calim had another way of tracking her, one she feared was magical. It was time to move on. She re-entered the cottage. Portan was sitting by the fire wrapped in a blanket.

"I have to move on. They found me and they will again. You aren't safe as long as I'm here. I hope you believe me now."

"You lied to me Yfrey. You aren't a harvester."

"No."

"I've never seen anything like your kind of power. What are you?"

"I'm The Conduit."

When she said the words the truth finally struck her. She was The Conduit. She had a mission. Portan looked at her in silence.

"I'll get my things and leave. I'm going to find their vehicles and destroy them. No-one will know they were here. You'll be safe."

The old man nodded.

Chapter Six

Since her last encounter, Jacques had been getting into shape. She would get up early and jog ten miles before breakfast. After breakfast she worked with weights and in the evening she had returned to her martial arts classes. She did not go for the training, her balance and precision she could work on alone. She went in order to spar. People were the unpredictable element in a fight and she wanted to hone her instincts along with everything else. She was feeling good. She was fitter than she had been in a long time, but still she used the deadbolt when she was in her flat alone and jumped at sudden noises. Ben insisted on picking her up from her evening classes and driving her home. She had not even made the pretence of objecting. She loved to run. Most mornings she was out of the flat before six o'clock and pounding the main street. Running this early was peaceful. Most people are still in bed or getting ready for work at this time and she could be alone with her thoughts and the streets.

It was a bright, crisp autumn morning and she was running extra hard. She no longer felt that the ten miles was challenging her and had decided to take a different path. If she cut through the park she could follow the path through an underpass and to a shopping area. Her new route followed a circuit, which meant that she did not have to stop and go back the way she came, she just had to keep going until she was back at her starting point.

Running along the main street she became aware of footsteps behind her. They seemed to be matching her pace. She felt an uncertainty rise up inside her throat. This was a public right of way. Of course others were allowed to run it too. Usually, setting out this early ensured solitude. She glanced over her shoulder to see who was flanking her. It was a man in a black jogging suit. The hood of his sweatshirt was up concealing his face. Anxiety turned into panic as the hooded figure followed her. She increased her pace as she turned off into the park, hoping that the stranger would take another route. He did not. Following her into the park, it seemed he too had increased his pace to maintain the distance between them. Jacques put her head down and powered towards the underpass. She would need to gain an advantage over this adversary. His pace increased with hers and he was getting closer. The underpass was ahead. She needed him closer anyway if this was going to work. He was not disappointing her, he was almost at her shoulder. She ran straight at the wall of the underpass, using her momentum to fly off it, serving up a roundhouse kick to the side of the man's head. He fell to the ground, stunned. Jacques assumed a defensive stance maintaining a safe distance from the man.

"Who are you? Why are you following me?"

"Jesus!" The man pulled down his hood revealing a bruised face. Jacques recognised him as the Karate instructor who taught the classes at the sports centre she attended.

"I'm sorry." She stepped forward and helped him to his feet. "I thought you were following me."

"I was."

"Why?"

"I wanted to talk to you."

"What about?"

"Do you want to go and get a coffee? This fast food place is open."

"O.K."

Jacques was still suspicious as she went for coffee with Paul. After all, if you want to talk to someone there are better ways to go about it than anonymously stalking them on their morning run. However, the fast food place already had a number of customers who had stopped in for breakfast before work, as well as several staff members milling around and as such, she felt it would be safer to talk to him here than to risk a less populated place. She took a seat whilst he bought the coffees. She leaned back against the chair to reassure herself that her dagger was still there, securely fastened between her shoulder blades by her sports bra. She had taken to carrying it with her. For some reason she did not feel right being without it. Its presence comforted her. When she jogged it was within easy reach –

smoothly drawn from its sheath if required – concealed by the upturned collar of her sports top. Every day before she set out for her jog she would practise drawing it. Should the occasion arise, she was ready.

Paul returned to the table carrying the coffees. As he placed them down in front of him he rubbed his jaw again.

"You've got quite a kick on you," he sounded impressed.

"I thought you were going to attack me."

"Do people usually attack you?"

"Only recently."

"Oh... well, I'm sorry. It must have seemed intimidating with my hood up. I didn't think. I'm prone to ear infections." After a pause he continued. "Is that why you came back to class? You were attacked? I mean, you certainly don't need the lessons."

"Yes, I wanted the sparring practice. I haven't for a while. Sparred, I mean."

"Well, that's what I wanted to talk to you about."

"Sparring?"

"Classes. My assistant is pregnant. She won't be able to teach with me now, it's unsafe for her. I was wondering if you'd step in. On a temporary basis I mean. It's £15 per hour, and I do four two hour sessions a week."

"Alright," Jacques agreed. The museum was only giving her half pay whilst she was on her 'leave of absence' and being paid whilst keeping in shape seemed to be just what she needed right now.

"I was going to talk to you at tonight's session," he continued, "but I saw you jogging whilst I was out on my morning run and thought I may as well just catch you then. I'm sorry if I frightened you, I didn't think."

"Well, I'm sorry I bruised your face, so guess we could call it even."

"That seems fair."

* * *

Jacques pounded home in record time. She was still not sure what to make of this chance encounter. She certainly did not believe in coincidences. She would be prepared for any eventuality. As she shut the door of her flat she reached over her shoulder and drew her dagger quickly and seamlessly. The presence of the blade in her hand felt totally natural, like the weapon was an extension of her. Using furniture to her advantage she traversed the flat expertly. If anyone were to attack her now they would have one hell of a fight on their hands. So why did she feel so terrified all the time? She was frightened to go to sleep. She did not like being alone. She had bought extra bolts for the front door and an early warning alarm system. Ben had offered to move in with her on a temporary basis – until she felt better. She had told him not to be so ridiculous. The slightest noise frightened her. She was a complete wreck, but would never admit it to her brother. She carefully sheathed her blade and put it down on the table in the living room. Picking up her weights she started pumping her arms up and down.

"I'm ready, let them come, I'm ready."

The mantra sounded certain. She was lying to herself and she knew it.

* * *

Before heading out to teach her first class Jacques had a shower and packed a gym bag. She wore her Karategi under her jacket, and had no intention of changing out of it when Ben picked her up at the end of the evening, but a bulging bag could quite easily conceal a dagger. She laid the sheathed blade on top of the outfit she had packed into the bag, placed a towel over it, then, headed out the door. Classes started at seven in the evening. It was now quarter to six. She wanted to get there early to help Paul set up and get herself warmed up. If she was being paid she wanted to earn her money. When she arrived Paul was sitting on the wall outside of the sports centre smoking a cigarette.

"You're early."

"Thought I'd help you set up."

"Awesome." He dropped the butt on the ground and stamped it out as he jumped down from his perch. He led the way into the sports centre. They quickly and effectively laid the mats out and Paul clipped the wooden edging together as Jacques tied the cover sheet down. They worked in companionable silence. When they were done Paul started to undress himself. He looked a bit embarrassed when he noticed Jacques' perplexed expression.

"I'm sorry. I'm used to doing this alone. I always change here before everyone arrives. I should find a toilet."

"It's a bit late for that," she said dryly. He had nothing to be ashamed of in terms of physique. His body was extremely well toned and the muscle definition in his arms and legs was impressive. Jacques found herself wondering how she had been so easily able to knock him off his feet.

"Sorry," he said again, turning his back on her in an attempt to preserve some sort of modesty. Starting between his shoulder blades and running down to the base of his spine was the tattoo of a cross. There were some symbols surrounding it that Jacques did not recognise.

"That's a nice tattoo."

"Thank you," he said as he pulled on his jacket and fastened his belt. "Do you want to spar before class arrives?"

"Sure." Jacques did a backflip onto the mats and assumed a defensive stance.

"Ha! O.K. then!" Paul did not attempt similar acrobatics, choosing instead to step onto the mat and bow.

The battle was intense. Clearly neither fighter was accustomed to losing and what should have been a simple warm up became very passionate very quickly. The two seemed well matched, blocking each other's attacks and landing an equal number of blows. Eventually Jacques took Paul's feet out from under him with a sweeping kick. She drew her fist back, and from a kneeling position thrust it at his face, stopping just before she made contact. The loud noise she made upon exhaling whilst completing this position told Paul that he was defeated.

"Ha!"

This final movement was accompanied by a round of applause from the gathered class who were standing at the edge of the mat waiting to be invited on. Jacques stood up awkwardly and reached down, pulling Paul to his feet. They bowed to each other and then to the class, who took the cue to step onto the mat.

"Well done." Paul spoke quietly as they took their positions at the front of the class and knelt down.

Two hours later class was over. It went very well. Jacques was good at teaching. Not a skill she would have credited herself with, as she was generally impatient with people. However, whether it was because they had witnessed her sparring with Paul, or whether it was because of the three white stripes on her black belt, the class seemed to respect her and paid careful attention to her advice. For her part she was able to see exactly where the flaws in her students' techniques were and help them to rectify them. In turn, she found watching those with poor technique helped to clarify in her own mind what was needed to improve hers.

When she had finished helping Paul pack the equipment away, he smiled at her and reached into the inside pocket of his jacket. Anxiety came over her. She took a step backwards. Her gym bag was on the other side of the room, and in it the dagger. In her mind she plotted the quickest course to the bag avoiding whatever weapon he was about to pull. It was his wallet. He took out £30 and held it out to her. She stepped forward and took the money, feeling a little foolish at her panic.

"Thanks."

"Thank you. That was an awesome session," he put his wallet back in his pocket. "Hey, it's still early. Do you want to maybe grab a drink? With me, I mean."

Jacques was taken aback. She had not seen this coming. Usually her general demeanour was enough to keep people away. This guy she had actually beaten up, twice, and he still liked her?

"That sounds nice," she began. "But my brother will be waiting outside for me in the car."

"O.K. Raincheck?"

"Sure."

"Great! I'll see you tomorrow then."

Before heading out into the dark, gravel car-park attached to the sports centre Jacques dived into the disabled toilet cubicle that was situated in the corridor which lead to the exit. Locking herself in, she unzipped her sports bag and retrieved her dagger. She tucked it into her belt and practised drawing it from its sheath several times until she was confident that she could do it with ease. She then pulled her coat on over the top to conceal the blade and exited the building, her kit bag slung over her shoulder.

The car-park was empty apart from a single car. It was Ben's clapped out old banger. Usually, when he saw her come out he would flash his lights at her, just in case she did not see him, or had trouble distinguishing his car from those that did not have their wing mirrors held on with string. Tonight the lights did not flash. Jacques became concerned. As she neared the car she could see that there was no-one in it. She put her bag down on the bonnet, unzipped the side pocket and pulled out her mobile phone. Scrolling down to Ben in the contacts list she pressed call. A ringing came from inside the car. She hung up. Now she was worried.

"Ben?" she called loudly into the darkness. The next thing she heard was a terrified scream. Without thinking she ran towards the noise.

Chapter Seven

Yfrey walked until dusk. She did not stop. Her priority was Portan's safety. She had not allowed herself to care about another person since her brother had been taken. Connections make you vulnerable. She should not have stayed so long with him. It had been against her better judgement, but the comfort of indoor living and regular meals had been so appealing. Now her presence had put Portan's safe, solitary existence under threat. She needed to fix her mistake; to make things safe for him again. Having spent the last three weeks in relative comfort, the rain was taking its toll and she felt more exhausted than she remembered feeling before. Maybe she was just noticing it more. As she approached the edge of the forest she saw the large military vehicle parked on the outskirts. The forest provided excellent cover. It was too dense for any of those land vehicles to penetrate. The magics that protected the forest meant that it could not be felled. Yfrey suspected that part of the reason for the inquisition was to eliminate the powers which protected the forests and the meadows and the rivers to make way for corporate development. Since Calim had forced his way to power government, policy was no longer available to the people and any speculation in this regard was quickly silenced.

Yfrey used her powers to make herself invisible against the trees. She scanned the area for guards. It was possible that the vehicles had been left unattended, but unlikely. Still, she could see no-one around, so decided to act fast. She stepped out from her shadowy protection, looked down at the earth, calling upon its energies. When she looked up the vehicle was gone, buried in the earth, but her energies were depleted. She was about to retreat back into the forest, when she heard the howl of dogs, accompanied by the sound of a horn. The hunt was out. She was weakened by the exertion required to bury a vehicle in the earth, and was not confident of her ability to conceal herself in the woods from dogs – their senses were more heightened than those of humans. She did not want to risk bringing them anywhere near Portan, so she made a decision. She started to run, in the open. Behind her, she could hear barking and it was getting nearer. She did not know if they had picked up her scent but she had to keep moving, she was in the open. The rain was beating down mercilessly upon her and the darkness was so utterly all-encompassing that she could not see where she was going. Her hope was that she would come upon a river or a stream in which she could masque her scent and hopefully escape. She was running too hard to focus her energies on anything other than the process of physical movement; her lungs burned as she gasped to inhale the cold damp air.

Ahead of her she could see a light. It flickered, covering the entire colour spectrum, like an iridescent rainbow. She forced her way forward towards the light. As she drew closer, it was almost as though the light were an ethereal presence shimmering, and somehow three dimensional. The light was almost hypnotic and Yfrey felt herself pulled towards it. She wanted to slow her run and examine it, attempt to determine its source. To her terror she realised that she could not slow down. The light was pulling her towards it faster and faster. Suddenly it was upon her. A feeling of being smothered engulfed her and she could not breathe. As quickly as the light had swallowed her, it spat her back out again. She landed heavily on the muddy grass. Gasping for air she struggled to her feet. She had to keep moving. The light which had captured her was no-where to be seen. It was as though it had never existed. Perhaps it had not. Perhaps a combination of fear and physical exhaustion had caused her to hallucinate the entire event. She heard barking. Time to keep moving. She turned to run, but the dog was upon her. A huge, black beast leapt at her, knocking her to the floor. Yfrey pushed at the creature, trying to push it off of her. The high pitched sound of a whistle came from somewhere in the darkness, beyond her view. It caused the animal's ears to prick up and it abandoned its quarry and ran away. The next thing she knew a light was flashing in her eyes, almost blinding her. She raised her hand against the glare. It was immediately lowered. Then came the sound of a woman's voice.

"Oh God! I'm so sorry! He thinks everyone's his friend. You know what labs are like; don't know their own strength. Are you hurt?"

"No." Confused, Yfrey struggled to her feet. The woman was large, and wearing strange, brightly coloured clothes, the type of which Yfrey had never seen before.

"Well, that's good," the woman started to fumble in a large sack she had been carrying. "I might have a towel in here for you to wipe the mud off yourself – I almost always take one on the walks – it's muddy this time of year. Still, at least it's not raining."

"No." Yfrey said again, suddenly realising that the rain had stopped.

"Dammit! I've always got a towel in here, where is it?"

"That's alright, I need to go."

"Well, at least take my number, I'll cover the cleaning bill on your outfit."

"No – I have to go." Yfrey walked away quickly. She did not understand this strange encounter. She did not know where she was. She felt that walking quickly would draw less attention to herself than running. Wherever she was, people did not seem afraid of her, so clearly did not know who she was. One thing was clear to her, the rain had stopped and she still had absolutely no idea what she was doing. She came to the edge of the field, to what seemed to be a street. It was like nothing she had ever seen before. The ground was grey and hard, and harsh bright lights atop giant poles made it seem desolate and terrifying. Three figures in black hoods were walking towards her, talking loudly and laughing. She hurried on, hoping they would not notice her. She came to a desolate field. The ground was made of the same grey substance the streets were, but it was not as smooth. Loose stones made walking difficult. She focused on the ground as she walked so as not to trip up. Still she stumbled. She landed hard on some sort of smooth shelf that gave a little with the weight of her impact and bounced up and down. Turning to the side to see what she had landed on, she saw a man looking out at her from within the structure. He was wearing the white collar and cross of an inquisitor. No, no, no, no, no, no, no! She thought desperately. Pushing herself to her feet she started to run. He had already opened the door of the structure and stepped out.

"Hey!"

She kept running. There was a massive black building in front of her that could perhaps provide some cover. As she skirted around the edge she tripped over something metal. She hit the ground hard. Her hands and knees stung, and whatever was in that container was all over her and stank of rotten food. Breathing heavily the inquisitor rounded the corner and saw her. He did not speak, just breathed.

"Stay away from me! I'm warning you!"

She raised her stinging hands to call upon the elements to protect her. Nothing happened. In utter despair she screamed.

Chapter Eight

Jacques arrived quickly at the location of the scream. Her new fitness routine had imbued her with both speed and stamina. Immediately she saw her overweight brother, leaning forward, grasping his knees and wheezing. Tucked behind a large metal skip that held the rubbish for the sports centre, there was, collapsed on the floor, a woman, so covered in blood and mud that she was barely recognisable, shaking in terror. Jacques assessed the situation immediately and shoved her brother angrily on the arm. The force of this unexpected jolt made him step sideways.

"Whatcha think you're doing moron? Breathing all over her like some sort of pervert!" Ben was only able to wheeze in response. "Jesus, you're so unfit! You need to start doing some sort of exercise or you're gonna be dead before you're forty."

She turned away from the sweaty mess that was her brother to the crumpled shaking woman amongst the rubbish.

"Hey, it's OK. I know that outfit makes him look ultra pervy, but he means well. If he weren't so ridiculously unfit he'd have told you that himself." She crouched down to be at eye level with the woman. "I'm Jacques, and that's my idiot brother, Ben. You're quite safe with us, I promise."

Yfrey looked at the woman who was crouching before her. Everything in this place was harsh, bright and hard. This woman too was strong. She had attacked the inquisitor without fear and he had supplicated to her will. Yfrey could barely make out her features in the darkness, but her eyes were bright and intense and something about them made her feel safe.

"I'm Yfrey," she spoke slowly, unsure whether the name would mean anything to these people.

"Evie?"

"I don't know where I am." Her voice cracked as she spoke, she had nearly lost control of her emotions completely. She was tired, sore, and bleeding. In a strange world where she did not have her powers, she was nothing.

"You're hurt; you can't stay here. Come with us and we'll get you cleaned up, it's OK, I promise." She gently reached down, put her hand under Yfrey's arm and helped her to her feet. Ben, still wheezing slightly made his way around to take her other arm.

"No!" Yfrey cried in panic, pulling away from him.

"It's OK." Jacques spoke reassuringly as she physically positioned herself between them. "Back off Ben, stay on this side of me."

Ben complied, giving his sister a concerned look as she continued to support Yfrey's elbow and walk her to the car.

"Do you think..." he began uncertainly.

"I do."

"Then we should take her straight to the police, let them deal with it."

"No! What the hell are they going to do? Poke and prod her, subject her to questions that she can't answer, make her feel more disgusting and violated than she already does. No, Ben – she comes home with me – she needs someone who understands."

"Jacques – that's – I mean – how could I possibly understand?"

"You didn't even try. You ran off into religion and hoped that God would explain it to you."

"I still pray for that Jacques."

"Don't waste your energy on my account, I'm fine." She turned to Yfrey who had been walking beside her, apparently unaware of the stage whispers argument that had been going on between the siblings. She was allowing herself to be led by this woman, whom she had never met before, to a place she had never been. Somehow it felt like the right thing to do. "This is it. It's a bit clapped out and stinks of petrol – but it's not far to my place."

"What is it?"

"Oh, a small flat above a garage. It's fine. Quite secure – I've alarms and deadbolts and..."

"No, that."

"Ben's car?"

"Car?"

"Ha! Yes! It used to be a hatchback in the early eighties, now I guess 'rust bucket' would be a more accurate description of it. When you consider that the church is the richest land owner in the country you'd think they could afford an upgrade for him."

"I mean, what is it? What does it do?"

Jacques turned and looked directly into Yfrey's eyes, she had wanted to maintain a distance and appear totally nonthreatening but this statement could imply a head injury. She studied her eyes intensely for signs of a concussion, variation in pupil size or staring into the distance. There was nothing, the eyes were bright blue, frightened, but open and innocent.

"A car. It's a vehicle. We sit inside and it carries us to our destination. Did you hit your head?"

"I don't know; I fell by the wall."

Jacques took Yfrey's head in her hands and felt around the matted mud encrusted hair for signs of cuts and bruises, still focusing intensely on her eyes.

"You seem fine." She concluded after what felt like an eternity. "Here, climb in, I'll help you strap yourself in."

"No! What are you doing?" Yfrey moved herself away from the seatbelt in panic.

"It's OK." Jacques immediately released the clip and backed away. "It's not far, it's OK."

"She has to strap in!" Ben objected.

"Aw, who the hell is gonna pull over a priest? And it's a five-minute drive."

"Jacques," he pulled his sister to one side and spoke in a confidential whisper, "she doesn't know what a car is. There's something mentally wrong with her. We need to take her to hospital."

"She's in shock. If we take her to any sort of institution, it'll only make things worse. You need to trust me on this."

"I do trust you, but I worry about you too. I'm allowed to worry about you."

"It's an utterly pointless pastime. Come on, drive me home."

They drove back to the flat in relative silence. The strange, toxic smell that emitted from the vehicle, combined with the horrific noise it made and the strange juddering sensation of its movement made Yfrey feel quite sick, and she focused her attention on the strange new world outside that was flying past her too quickly to take in. They stopped outside a grey building with an angry looking metal staircase up the outside of it.

"Here we are then, home sweet home." Jacques attempted to sound cheery. It was not something she did often and as a result it sounded forced and awkward.

"Do you want me to come up with you?" Ben offered, throwing a suspicious glance towards Yfrey.

"No, don't exhaust yourself, we'll be fine."

"Well, I'll pop in tomorrow and check in on you."

"Could you maybe bring some clothes? That outfit should go straight in the bin, it's beyond saving."

"I'll bring some money – you can buy her some. That's what the poor box is for after all."

"Thanks Ben."

"Look after yourself." He looked at her seriously.

"We'll be fine, promise."

With that Jacques leapt out of the car, slung her sports bag over her shoulder and hurried round to the driver's side back door, which Yfrey had been pushing at with little success. She pulled the handle and opened it from the outside.

"Don't worry, that one always sticks." She offered her hand to help Yfrey from the car, but it was refused. "It's just at the top of the stairs." She indicated the metal staircase which led up to the flat. Yfrey shielded her eyes against the bright security light which had flashed on as the car pulled up.

"Everything is so harsh here," she began weakly.

"I know it feels that way..." Jacques trailed off. There was nothing of comfort that she would be able to offer which was true, and she had never been a good liar. "Follow me." She led the way up the steps without offering further physical assistance or making any attempts at conversation. As they entered the flat Jacques hit the light switch that was on the inside wall. Yfrey quickly raised her hands to protect her eyes again, and just as quickly Jacques turned it off.

"I'm sorry." She opened the top drawer of the telephone table, which sat against the wall of the hallway and produced a torch. The yellow light which it emitted was soft and dim. "I keep it in case of power cuts," she offered by way of an explanation.

Yfrey just stared at her blankly. She could feel the tears welling up inside her. She had not cried, not since her brother had been taken – but this place was strange and horrible. Hard and fierce. This woman with the unusual markings and kind eyes had a stick that made light with no fuel or fire. She used words that Yfrey did not understand and no-one was ever kind without an agenda. This woman's agenda was unclear.

"Come on, you'll want to have a bath, I'll show you the bathroom."

Yfrey allowed herself to be led by the light of the metal stick to the bathroom. Once there Jacques lay the stick down on some sort of shelf which contained strange objects.

"OK." Jacques put her hands behind her head awkwardly as she spoke. The gesture was unnatural and Yfrey took a step away from her, unsure what would happen next. "So," she continued. "It's pretty basic. You got your toilet, sink, bath is pretty standard. You'll have to run the hot tap a while before it warms up. Help yourself to bubbles. Towels are in the airing cupboard there; use the bathrobe on the door when you're done, it's clean and I'll see if I can sort you out a pair of PJs, OK?" She went to leave but Yfrey caught her arm weakly.

"I don't know what to do. I've never been in a place like this before." She felt utterly helpless and out of her depth.

"Are you sure you didn't hit your head?"

"This is not my world! I don't know how I came here, but it's horrible and hard and bright and totally unnatural!" Her voice was beginning to crack under the emotional strain. "I'm not insane, but I can't prove anything I say. I have no powers here." With this last statement she collapsed on the floor in tears. Jacques crouched down and placed her hands awkwardly on her knees.

"OK, look; this is a toilet. You sit on it here when you need to, um, expel waste. Then you push that handle there and it cleans it away for you. The bath, you fill up with warm water and sit in it to clean the dirt off yourself.

Come on, I'll help you fill it. Come here, you can tell me when it's hot enough."

Yfrey stood awkwardly and made her way to the bath. Jacques turned on the taps and ran her hand under them.

"Right, it's starting to warm up. I'm putting the plug in, see? When you're done you pull it out and the water drains away. I'll put some bubbles in." She started to stir the water with her arm. "Here, come feel if this is a good temperature for you."

Yfrey tentatively put her hand in the bubbly water and withdrew it again quickly. It was warm to the touch and the texture of the white bubbles tickled and crackled against her skin in a way that was most unusual.

"How do you make it warm without a fire?"

"I have a boiler behind the wall. Not a good boiler – in fact, this degree of tepid is about as good as it gets. I generally boil the kettle to wash up." She drifted off. It was clear from Yfrey's expression that washing up and kettle were also foreign words to her. "OK, well that's enough water. I'll leave you with your privacy. Just throw your clothes straight in that bin there – there's nothing we can do for them. As I say, the bathrobe on the door is clean. I'll go make the sofa up for you. So. Yeah." She hastened out of the room, shutting the door behind her.

Yfrey was alone in the room. There was a small bolt on the inside of the door, which would be totally ineffective against anyone trying to break in. She slid it across anyway. She removed The Book of Abisan from one of the folds in her dress. Carefully she lifted the stick light up and placed the book underneath it. Then she undressed herself. Her clothes were heavy from the rain and mud that entrenched them. With no clothes she felt how much of a weight on her they had been. Next, she tried the odd looking toilet. She had never seen anything like it, shiny and high off the ground, like a throne. She pushed the handle and watched in amazement as a gush of water took everything away with it, leaving a clean white bowl. Then she tried dipping a foot in the warm water. It was an interesting tickly sensation. She stepped back. Fumbling about in the pile of dirty clothing she extracted her knife and placed it on the side of the bath next to her before allowing herself to sink into the warm suds.

Chapter Nine

Yfrey's hair was long. Cutting it had never been a priority whilst she had been on the run. As a result, it was extremely matted and utterly coated in mud. She lay back in the warm soapy water, allowing it to cover her entire face apart from her nose. The bubbles tickled, but she could feel the weight of her hair tearing at her scalp, pulling her down. She felt like she was being strangled by its oppressive presence on her head. Reaching for her knife she sawed away at it until it was no longer a part of her. She held the mat of hair before her. Suddenly she felt engulfed by an immense relief and she started to cry.

Jacques had hunted the entire flat and had managed to find the massive bag of tea-lights that she kept in case of a power outage. Having seen Yfrey's reaction to electric lighting she thought it best to avoid it for the time being. Having sorted through all of her spare bedding she had managed to find a pair of old grey jogging bottoms and a sweatshirt which would have to serve as an outfit until she could get Yfrey to the shops tomorrow. She looked so undernourished that even tying the drawstring as tight as possible Jacques wondered if the trousers would not fall down. She was just finishing putting the bedding on the sofa when she heard the bathroom door close and looked up. Yfrey was before her, wearing the white bathrobe. In her hand she was holding what looked like a dead rat. Her hair, which Jacques had assumed was brown was in fact extremely bright white and her blue eyes glowed stark against it.

"I had to cut it off, it was strangling me."

"I totally understand, but did you need to keep it as a pet? There's a bin in the bathroom."

Yfrey looked sheepishly at the floor and Jacques reached down and retrieved the waste paper basket from next to the sofa, offering it as a vessel with which to dispose of the offending object.

"How did you cut it off? I don't keep scissors in the bathroom."

"I have a knife." Yfrey removed her blade from the dressing gown pocket and offered it handle first to Jacques.

Taking it Jacques examined the weapon closely. The handle was a dull bronze with a comfortable grip and the blade itself was slightly curved. It did not feel like her knife: that felt as though it had been made especially for her. This was a foreign object. She handed it back without speaking. Yfrey had been staring at her the whole time and now she spoke.

"Your hair is not supposed to be that colour."

"Ha! You can talk! What's that serious peroxide job you've got going on?"

"All my people's hair is this colour." She did not know what it was about Jacques that she trusted – but she felt totally unafraid with her.

"Oh, I'm sorry, I didn't mean to be personal. Do you want to look at my knife whilst I make us a cup of tea?" Jacques had absolutely no idea where this last question came from. She had never had strong conversational skills, but offering someone a look at a deadly weapon she had been carrying around was not something even her limited people skills deemed acceptable. Now the offer had been made though so she removed her coat and took the ornate sheathed blade from her belt before offering it to Yfrey. Then she retreated to the kitchen to boil the kettle.

As soon as Yfrey touched the blade she felt its power surge through her. This blade had magical roots. She seated herself on the sofa and placed the blade on the coffee table. Removing The Book of Abisan from her dressing gown pocket she flicked through it until she found what she was looking for: a picture of a knife. Underneath the image it read:

"The Blade of Conquetis. In the right hands this weapon is one of the most powerful tools a witch can possess. There is only one in existence and it has been lost for generations. It is said that when the blade is found, The Roghnaithe will arise from the darkness and lead us all to victory."

Jacques entered carrying two mugs of steaming liquid. She placed the mugs on the coffee table and seated herself next to Yfrey.

"Is that a picture of my knife?"

"I think so."

"What book is that? What language is it in?"

"My language."

"Is English not your first language?"

"What do you mean?" After a pause Yfrey reached out and touched the nape of Jacques' neck tentatively. "Who branded you?"

"It's not a brand, it's a tattoo, I wanted it."

"Why? Are you a warrior? Is that why you wear the war paint?"

Jacques laughed weakly. "In a way I guess it is war paint. It's to tell people not to mess with me. Fat lot of good it's done me lately."

"What do you mean?"

"Oh, nothing. I've just had some unpleasant experiences lately. It doesn't matter." She held her mug of tea tightly in her hands and stared intensely into the steam.

"You are a warrior, I can tell. You're strong. That is a warrior's weapon. It has great power and it chose you."

"I don't know if it chose me – someone posted it to me. Was all a bit random really, but I wouldn't be without it now, it makes me feel safe. I can't really explain it, it's just a feeling I have."

"When I touched it, it made me realise that there is magic in this world, it's just on a different frequency. I can get my powers back."

"Your powers?"

"There's magic in everything, we just need to learn how to channel it. You need to believe that or you'll lose yourself." She gently reached out and took Jacques' hand looking into her eyes. She had seemed so strong when she was with the inquisitor but now there was something very vulnerable about her.

"I don't know if I can believe in anything other than myself. Sometimes I envy Ben so much. What happened…" as she spoke she found her grip on Yfrey's hand tightening. She did not know what it was about this woman that made her open up, but she felt safe talking to her. "What happened made his faith stronger – he looked to God for answers. I couldn't believe in a god who had abandoned me – left me to the mercy of that, that monster. I realised that the only person I could rely on was me – so I learned Karate and got my war paint," she smiled weakly at this joke and glanced up from her tea to meet Yfrey's eye. "Ben never gave up on me. He just doesn't know what to do or say. Still, after all this time things between us are awkward. I think it's partly my fault."

Yfrey matched the tightness of the grip on her hand. She felt very protective of this woman whom she had only just met and she did not know why. She knew that she would never let anything happen to her and she needed her powers back to ensure it. The key was in the knife, she needed to channel its energy.

"Ben is your brother?"

"Yes, my hapless brother. What about you? Do you have brothers or sisters?"

"I had a brother – Torius."

"Had? Oh – I'm sorry. What happened to him?"

"Like your brother he was very protective of me. Unlike your brother he was of a naturally violent disposition. Our people are gentle. We live in harmony with the world around us. He wanted to be a force. He was very angry. It was his anger that destroyed him in the end I think. I'm not saying we shouldn't fight back. We should protect what is ours. But we shouldn't let a drive for hatred and anger motivate us. Even if we win our fight we lose ourselves in the process – and then, what have we really won? I haven't stopped running since I lost Torius. I'm exhausted."

"I'm sorry. I should leave you to sleep."

"No, please. Stay with me – I find your presence comforting. I can't explain it, it's like I've known you forever."

"I know."

Chapter Ten

Ben hurried down the steps to his car. He was concerned. Opportunistic rapists were unlikely to dress as priests, which led him to the disturbing conclusion that it was one of his own brethren responsible the attack. He managed to start the car on the third attempt and drove as quickly as was safe to St Michael's. Father Frederick would know what to do. He parked awkwardly across two spaces and hurried down the gravel path to the vast gothic building that he had called home for so many years. The exertion of hurrying meant that his entry into the building was accompanied by heavy wheezing which could have disturbed the prayers of a less pious man than Father Frederick, who knelt at the lectern unmoved by the breath sounds that echoed around the large empty building. Ben crossed himself upon entering the church. So distracted was he as he made his way in that he knocked into a precarious pile of hymn books which subsequently tumbled to the ground. As he awkwardly stooped to pick up the fallen books, Father Frederick, eventually distracted from his prayers by the sudden noise looked up to see what was going on.

"Ben? What are you doing here? I thought you were visiting your sister tonight. Did you quarrel again?"

"No, Father. I have been given some information that has upset me and I wanted to talk to you about it."

"But of course. Come into my office and we can talk."

Father Fredrick rose from his kneeling position and crossed to the back of the church. He ducked behind a curtain and headed down the long corridor to where his office was located. The room was large, with a large old oak desk, ornately carved. Religious icons adorned the walls in massive gold frames and the book case at the back of the room contained many old volumes.

Taking a seat and indicating that Ben should do the same, Father Frederick poured himself a glass of whiskey and offered the bottle to Ben, who declined.

"So, what is it that is troubling you?"

"Father, my sister has a friend staying with her."

"A female friend?"

"Yes."

"I suspected as much of your sister. I understand that you may find this troubling, but she is a very lost young woman. We can only hope and pray that she finds her way back to The Lord."

"No! Not that kind of friend!"

"Oh, I'm sorry. So, what's troubling you?"

"Her friend was attacked by men dressed as priests. Why would priests want to attack anyone?"

"Well, they wouldn't, it was probably people dressed up for a stag party, you know, one last fling before marriage."

"Rape is not a fling Father!"

"You said attacked, not raped." Father Frederick corrected him firmly.

"What? Just because I didn't spell it out doesn't mean it's alright. I don't understand the relevance of that semantic."

"I can guarantee that your sister's friend was not raped, and if that is what she told you then she is a liar."

"She didn't say that, but how do you know?" Ben was starting to get suspicious of Father Frederick. He had never known the priest be this definite about anything and his certainty worried him.

"You seem awfully certain it wasn't priests," Ben began uncertainly. "I think perhaps I was over reacting, I should go and get some sleep." He started to notice Father Frederick's continual nervous glances towards the bookcase. Was there something there that should not be? "After all, you're absolutely right, why would a priest want to hurt anyone?"

"No, indeed. Well, you'd better get home, you've upset yourself enough for one night. I know you think you're being charitable by spending so much time with your sister, but she's making you unhappy. Maybe it's time to think about yourself." Father Frederick looked again to the bookcase, this time Ben followed his gaze and his eyes fell on the spine of a very old book. There was no writing indicating what it was, just a cross branded into the side.

"Father," Ben said, suddenly making a decision. "Could I borrow that Bible? I loaned mine to Jacques in the hope she would find some comfort in its words, and there is a passage I want to look up." As he spoke he rose to his feet and reached to take the book down from the shelf. It came out half way, then jammed. To Ben's utter astonishment the shelf moved away revealing a secret passage. "What on Earth is this?" "Ben, you know what curiosity did to the cat, and you don't have nine lives. I love parables, you can say things without actually saying them."

"I think it's too late to warn me off now Father. You clearly know more than you have been prepared to reveal to me. I think it was priests who attacked Evie and I think you're trying to cover it up. Now you can tell me what you know and try to explain it to me or I will go to the police and tell them what I know."

"What do you know? That a woman who doesn't exist in this world as far as they know was attacked by someone dressed as a priest. That there is a secret passage in the back of my office that leads to the cellar? Lots of old buildings have secret passages; they stem back from before the civil war when Catholicism was outlawed. The police will laugh you out the door."

"There is something down there you don't want me to see!" Ben suddenly made the decision and hurried down the steps to the basement.

"Ben!" Father Frederick called after him. "Once you've seen it there's no going back!"

At the bottom of the stairs, Ben was met with the most amazing glowing light. It was at the back of the room, shimmering and iridescent. It seemed to sing a song that only he could hear. For a moment he felt totally at peace.

"What is it?" Ben asked in total amazement.

"It's a portal to another world." Father Frederick had followed him down and was now at his side.

"What?"

"I told you there was no going back once you had seen it. Sometimes it's too much for the human mind to grasp, people go completely mad. I'd hate to see you committed." There was a sinister tone to his voice now.

"Don't worry about me Father. Part of being a Catholic is believing that things exist that are beyond our understanding. It would be vain to assume that this was the only world that God, in all his infinite wisdom had created. There is a massive universe out there, we can't be the only life in it. That does not explain why priests attacked Evie. Are you saying it wasn't priests, but people from this 'other world'? If they are coming through and hurting people surely we have a responsibility to stop them?"

"They are not hurting people, Ben, unless those people were, say, the instrument of the Devil." Suddenly Father Frederick's expression became very dark.

"What do you mean the instrument of the Devil? Evie is no such thing. She is a gentle soul, I can tell."

"It's possible that Evie has bewitched you."

"No, it isn't. What are you saying?"

"We are very lucky here, magic no longer exists. But in this world, where I was born and raised there are still the abominations known as witches."

"What are you talking about Father? Magic isn't real! Evie is not an abomination; she is a sweet girl. She would never hurt anyone."

"The Devil can hide his face, Ben. That's why he has survived so long. Yfrey has to be terminated. She threatens the harmony of both our worlds. I can't expect you to understand now, but hopefully you will eventually."

"And Jacques? What did she threaten? Working in her basement every day, she wasn't bothering anyone!"

"Why do you think the witch is here, Ben? Your sister is the downfall of civilisation as we know it. I was hoping not to involve you in this, as family can be complicated, but I can't have you interfering with my work. You are either with me or against me I'm afraid."

"Then I'm against you! I can't allow you to hurt my sister."

"What about all the innocent people your sister is threatening? An entire way of life will be destroyed if she is allowed to succeed with her plan."

"You are insane." Ben turned towards the stairs to leave.

"I'm sorry Ben, I can't have you interfering. I hope you'll understand one day." Father Frederick smashed the whiskey bottle over Ben's head knocking him unconscious. He dragged him to the back of the basement and bound his hands to his feet with his belt. Then he ascended the stairs to conduct Mass.

Chapter Twelve

Paul was as pleasant and friendly as always before and during class. He made small talk and joked with Jacques, but not once did he mention dinner. She was beginning to wonder if he had changed his mind. Once the mats had been packed away she picked up her bag and awkwardly began to head for the door.

"Is your brother picking you up?"

"No, I told him I had a lift tonight."

"Dinner and a lift?"

"Yes."

"Excellent!"

"Let me just go change."

"Cool."

Jacques made her way towards the disabled toilet. She felt intense anxiety in the pit of her stomach. It had been there since the first attack, but she had found that sticking to her strict exercise regime had managed to suppress it. Now she felt distinctly unsettled, almost guilty. As she tucked Yfrey's knife into her belt and pulled her top down to cover it she brushed the feelings aside. She had not been on a date in, what seemed like, forever. That must be it, pre-date nerves. She was going to be fine.

When she emerged from her changing room Paul was waiting outside for her. He looked very handsome in his black long-sleeved shirt and dark blue jeans with leather belt and black boots. When he saw her he smiled broadly.

"No Goth makeup tonight?"

"Tonight I'm not at war."

"Strange thing to say, are you usually?"

"I think I felt I ought to be, or something. My friend, the one staying with me described it as my war paint. She has a totally innocent way of putting things so that they make perfect sense."

"She doesn't mind you leaving her tonight?"

"Ben's taken pizza round. She didn't mind anyway; I was just worried about leaving her. She's had some bad experiences recently. But she's strong, stronger than you can imagine."

"I'd like to meet her; it sounds like you are very close."

"I feel like I've known her forever. Maybe we could all go out for a drink tomorrow?"

"I would like that very much," Paul said, still smiling broadly. "So, Chinese or Italian?"

"I think Chinese. I can wow you with my unbelievable skill with a chopstick."

"I'm already wowed by you, now I'm in awe. I always have to ask for a fork."

Jacques blushed as they entered the restaurant. Paul held the door open and pulled out her chair for her to sit down. The waitress smiled as she handed them the menus and asked, "Can I get you anything to drink?"

"Just water for me, thank you," Paul smiled, "I'm driving."

"Could I have a vodka and tonic please?"

"Absolutely you can. I'll be back in a jiff to take your order," the waitress beamed emphatically.

Jacques felt non-plussed. The waitress had just treated her like a normal person. With Paul she felt normal. She had not felt normal in as long as she could remember. In her view her makeup and attire was an outward projection of her inner self. Now, here she was with this handsome man who was genuinely interested in her and what she had to say. Everyone around them in the restaurant was laughing and joking, and, so were she and Paul. They blended in.

"Well," Paul said as he helped her on with her coat at the end of the evening. "Where to now?"

"I had better get home, Evie will be wondering where I am. But I would love to introduce you to her over drinks tomorrow, if you'd still like to, that is."

"I would very much like to – she obviously means a great deal to you – I can tell by the way you talk about her. In case I haven't made it clear yet, I have had a wonderful time tonight."

"So have I, thank you for asking me."

He held the car door open for her as she climbed in. It was not a long drive back to her flat and she found herself wishing it was further. As they pulled in the searing security light attached to the garage came on illuminating the occupants of the car under its bright glow.

"Well, thank you for a lovely evening. May I walk you to your door?"

"You may." Jacques could not stop grinning as Paul followed her up the steps to the door. She would invite him in for coffee, she thought. As she turned the key in the door and opened it, he spun her around and kissed her.

"What's this?" He asked, his hand was resting on the knife in her belt.

"Promise you won't laugh?"

"Of course."

"It's my knife."

"Ha! You carry a knife?"

"For protection, yeah."

"Can I see it?"

"Sure," Jacques drew Yfrey's knife from her belt and handed it to him handle first. Upon seeing the knife Paul's expression changed, rather than eager and mildly amused it now seemed angry and frustrated.

"This is not your knife."

"What do you mean?"

"Where did you get this?"

"My friend gave it to me." Jacques was confused by the change in tone and the abrupt nature of the questioning.

"Don't lie to me!" Paul had started to wield the knife threateningly. "Where is YOUR knife?"

"What is wrong with you?" Jacques was suddenly equally annoyed. "Give my knife back." She grabbed at the knife but he held it out of reach.

"Foolish woman! Giving up your only defence; pathetic! Tell me where you got this blade and where yours is or I will gut you like a fish!"

Jacques felt her cheeks redden with a sense of anger and betrayal, but she had no time to experience or understand the emotions, she needed to react.

"Not my only weapon!" She kicked him in the stomach and hurried inside. She tried to close the door behind her, but he had already used Yfrey's blade to prevent this from happening. Jacques stumbled into the living room in total panic. Yfrey was sitting on the chair, still holding the knife in both hands. She opened her eyes upon hearing Jacques enter and looked at her.

"Evie, we're in trouble!"

"Understatement of the year," Paul mocked as he barged in after her, then he stopped. "Yfrey?"

"Torius? I thought you were dead! What are you doing here?" As she spoke she rose to her feet, not to greet her brother, but to gently move Jacques behind her and act as a protective barrier between the two of them.

"Yfrey! You found the blade! I knew this woman had it. I have been trying to seduce it away from her, but you already have it! I could have saved myself the trouble."

"That's my knife."

"Yes," he handed the blade back to Yfrey. "I thought she must have killed you for it."

"I gave it to her."

"Why?"

"Because I want her to be safe."

"Evie?" Jacques spoke nervously. "What's going on? What language are you speaking?"

"Can't you understand me? It's the same language I have always spoken to you."

"It's not, it sounds like Gaelic or something."

"She can't understand us when we speak to each other because we don't want her to. Speaking to her, her understanding us becomes a necessity. It's one part of our magic that still works in this awful world." Torius explained impatiently.

"I want her to understand me always."

"Then she will," he retorted petulantly. "This would have gone much smoother if she couldn't understand us."

“What are you doing Torius?”

“Thomas? Your brother?” Jacques was becoming more and more confused.

“Yes. Please trust me and stay behind me. And hold this.” She returned Jacques her blade.

“What are you doing? I need that if I am ever to face Calim.”

“It’s the blade of the Roghnaithe, Torius, it will not work for you.”

“What do you know? You lock yourself away with your books and your prophecies; you don’t know the slightest thing about war.”

“I know about killing. I know that each time you take a life, no matter how hateful that life is, a part of your humanity dies with it. I know that I was utterly lost until she found me. I know that she is a true warrior; she has met with so much adversity and is still strong. Tonight I have studied the book and the blade and know that she is the Roghnaithe, and I will not let you touch her.”

“You think you can stop me? You have no powers here and physically I am by far your superior.”

“I know I can, it is written that I must.”

“Written? You think you’re the Conduit? Yfrey, these prophecies are insane. You know that only force can stop Calim.”

“If it’s so insane then why do you need her knife?”

“Yfrey, I have been searching for this knife too long to let the fact that it is in the possession of your only friend ever stop me from getting it. Now, you can either tell her to hand it over, or I can take it, forcibly, but either way I’m leaving with it.”

“Do you really think you can take it from me?” Jacques, who had been listening in silence to the exchange now spoke. “We both know you can’t best me in a combat situation. That’s why you tried to seduce me. Trying to take it by force didn’t work out so well for you in the underpass did it? So you thought you’d regroup, try a new approach. You aren’t getting anything from me tonight.”

Torius took a flick knife from his pocket, clearly one he had acquired in this world and moved menacingly towards Jacques.

“Torius!” Yfrey called her brother’s name but looked beyond him to the huge figure that now loomed in the doorway. It was the giant man who had attacked Jacques in the basement, and he had a gun.

“Please don’t let me interrupt you. If you kill each other it’ll save me the trouble.”

“Kemp!” Torius turned abruptly. “How the hell did you find me?”

“Still that same arrogance that led to all your followers dying, Torius? I’m not looking for you, you are nothing anymore. No army, no followers, just one pathetic man holding onto a vision. I am here to kill the Roghnaithe. And I see the Conduit is here too, so I’ll soon be able to get out of this awful place and be welcomed home a hero. Now, if you get out of my way you won’t be hurt.”

“Yfrey, RUN!” As he spoke Torius leapt at Kemp grabbing his gun hand. The two men wrestled and the gun went off. Yfrey turned to Jacques, her eyes were wide and her face was pale.

“Evie, I’ve been shot.”

Yfrey looked at the blood that was starting to pool through the shoulder of Jacques’ cream top.

“Go! I’ll find you!” Torius repeated as he and Kemp continued to grapple.

“Come on, we need to move.” Yfrey took Jacques by the hand and hurriedly led her out of the flat.

Chapter Thirteen

Yfrey literally dragged Jacques down the steps without looking back. Jacques was injured and in no condition to fight a trained soldier and Yfrey was still unsure of her powers in this world.

"Look," Jacques gasped as she struggled to keep up with Yfrey. "Paul left his keys in his car."

"Can you drive it?"

"I'll have to."

"We need to stop you bleeding."

"We need to get out of here first or my shoulder will be the least of our worries." She struggled into the car and started the engine.

"We should get you to a healer." Yfrey spoke urgently as she ripped the leg from the martial arts trousers that were strewn on the back seat and pressed the cloth hard against the wound.

"We can't go to hospital, it's a gunshot wound, they'll have to call the police. We aren't far from the supermarket; we can get supplies there."

Painfully Jacques put the car into gear and pulled out into traffic. Yfrey maintained pressure on the injury and watched Jacques intensely in an attempt to ascertain her condition. They parked awkwardly across two spaces.

"Check the glove compartment, I think he put his wallet in there," Jacques instructed. She turned and removed the black suit jacket from the hanger in the back of the car. She visibly winced as she pulled it on to conceal her bloodstained clothes. Yfrey touched her arm gently. She was terribly concerned and did not really know what to do.

"I'm fine. What has he got in his wallet?" Yfrey handed the black leather wallet over to Jacques. "Over £100. That'll be alright. Come on." She struggled out of the car and headed towards the entrance. Yfrey kept her hand lightly on her back, hoping that she could feed some of her energies into Jacques and keep her strong.

"Grab a basket." Jacques indicated the stack of baskets outside the main entrance. Yfrey picked one up and looked to Jacques for further instruction. "Come on, I know what we need." She headed to the pharmacy/cosmetics aisle and indicated the first aid kit, extra bandages and antiseptic hand cleaner. "OK, I'm gonna need a clean outfit and some booze to clean the wound." As they walked through the home aisle Jacques also threw some towels into the basket. "Booze is gonna be a problem because they'll want to see ID and neither of us have any."

"ID for what?"

"To prove we're over twenty-five."

"I can do that, just give me the money."

Jacques handed over the wallet and glanced quizzically at Yfrey who took the money and the basket and walked confidently up to the till. Smiling at the sales assistant she paid for the goods and returned to Jacques.

"What now?"

"How did you do that?"

"I projected an image of myself that appeared to clearly be over twenty-five. It's hard to explain how I do it – I wasn't sure I even could here, but I think I managed to channel some energy from your knife. What now?"

Jacques' knees buckled and she reached out to Yfrey for support. "There's toilets. Get me to the disabled one and we'll deal with it there."

Yfrey helped Jacques to the toilet and locked them both in. Jacques fell forward onto Yfrey.

"I'm sorry, I don't think I'm going to be much help to you."

"That's alright, I know what to do." Yfrey pulled the big beach towel out of the bag and lay it down on the floor. Jacques lowered herself onto it and struggled to take off her jacket. Her cream top was blood drenched and clinging to her. It was much worse than Yfrey had expected, but she did not react. Drawing her knife from her belt she cut the shirt away. As she removed it from the site of the wound Jacques made a whimpering noise from the pain.

"Here, bite down on this." Yfrey offered Jacques the leather sheath to her blade which she took and bit down on, hard. Yfrey unscrewed the lid of the vodka bottle and poured a serious amount over both sides of Jacques' shoulder before pressing another towel down hard on both sides of the wound. "It looks like the bullet went straight through, so I won't have to retrieve it." She tried to sound relaxed and confident as she spoke, but she was concerned by the amount of blood Jacques had lost. After applying pressure and the towel for some time, the bleeding subsided significantly enough for her to remove the towel and apply the dressings from the first aid kit. She taped the dressings over both sides of the shoulder then bandaged diagonally across the body. The new top they had bought was a large black, men's zip up hoodie. It was very big and baggy and concealed the otherwise noticeable padding over Jacques' shoulder. When it was done Jacques fell forward towards the toilet bowl and vomited. Yfrey bagged up the bloodstained clothes and rags and pushed them down hard into the big yellow bin in the corner of the room. Supporting Jacques as best she could, she helped her to her feet.

"Come on, we need to get you somewhere you can rest."

"I can't drive again, I can't even see straight, and we can't go back to mine, he'll be waiting."

"I saw an inn advertising rooms just behind this building, we can go there."

"They'd want a credit card, and we don't have one."

"Those plastic cards? There are three in Torius' wallet."

"Neither of us look like a six foot two man called Paul."

"I will, to whoever needs to see me that way."

"Wow, OK."

Booking a room was easy. For some reason the young woman behind the desk simply swiped the card without asking for a signature or a pin number, although it was likely that Yfrey would have had a contingency in place should this have happened. Jacques was very weak by this point and Yfrey virtually had to carry her to the lift.

"Press the up arrow." Jacques instructed as she clung weakly to her friend. The doors opened and they made their way into the tiny mirrored box. It was small and claustrophobic but fortunately they were only on the second floor and they did not have to stay in it long.

"You know," Jacques said, trying to sound relaxed, "that receptionist was totally flirting with you, so much so that she didn't ask you to sign or anything."

"Torius always was attractive to the ladies."

"It is so weird. She actually saw you as him. Could I see you as somebody else if you wanted me to?"

"Yes. Do you want me to appear to you as someone else?"

"No. This is us."

Yfrey helped Jacques to the bed. She took a carton of the complimentary squash that was next to the kettle and handed it to Jacques.

"You should drink something and get some rest."

Obediently Jacques drank and lay back on the bed. She was too weak to fight anymore.

"Are you going to rest too?"

"I will. There is something I need to do first."

"OK." Jacques lay back and closed her eyes. Yfrey gently covered her with a blanket and watched her until she was certain that she was asleep. Then, she retrieved The Book of Abisan from her pocket and laid it down in front of her. If Jacques could not seek out a healer in this world then she would need to take her to Portan. Yfrey drew a circle in the bed linen with her finger and watched it rise up into the air and form a golden orb in front of her.

"Show me the way back," she commanded.

Chapter Fourteen

Yfrey had a location. She knew how to return to her world. Jacques was in no condition to fight though, which meant that she would have to do some reconnaissance alone. It was still dark and now was the best time. She gently brushed Jacques' hair out of her face and waited for her to open her eyes.

"I have to go out, there's something I need to do."

"Hold on, I'll come with you."

"No, you stay here. You're injured and I'll be quicker without you. I'll take the key so don't let anyone in, and please don't leave the room until I come back."

"Alright." Jacques was too weak and tired to argue so she simply closed her eyes again.

Yfrey slipped quietly out of the room. She knew exactly where she needed to be. Moving swiftly and silently through the dark streets she followed the path of lights that only she could see. She arrived at a huge, dark, gothic building. In its surroundings flat rectangular stones were jutting out of the ground. There was an immense wooden door at the front, but the lights told her she must go around the side, which she duly did. There was a small window at ground level which swung open on a broken latch. Through it she could see the same beautiful, shimmering portal which had first brought her to this strange world. She could feel strong magic emanating from it. All she had to do was get Jacques here and she had a pathway home. However, there was no way of knowing where the portal came out, and she did not wish to emerge in the middle of Calim's dining room. She would have to get a bit closer and investigate. She climbed through the open window feet first and lowered herself carefully to the ground. There was a loud crashing and grunting coming from the corner of the room. Drawing her blade she turned abruptly to see Ben, hog tied and gagged. She hurried to him and cut the gag from his mouth.

"Evie! How did you find me?"

"I wasn't looking for you," she whispered as she cut through his bonds. "I was looking for that."

"Why?" Ben asked as he pulled himself to a seated position and rubbed his wrists and ankles in an attempt to restore circulation to them.

"Jacques has been shot, I need to get her to a healer."

"You need to get her to a hospital, help me up, we'll call an ambulance."

"She will be vulnerable in one of your hospitals, surely you can see that?"

Ben looked beyond her to where Father Frederick was now standing. "Look out! Behind you!"

Yfrey turned sharply and dodged the cosh that was destined for the back of her skull.

"That's close enough Molek." Her voice was firm and had adopted a tone that Ben had not heard her use before.

"Yfrey. I'm honoured that you remember me. How is your brother?"

"He was fine the last time I saw him. Arrogant as ever, thinks he can take you all on alone."

"He's still alive?" Father Frederick was clearly shaken by this news and had been put on the defensive. "Well, let's hope he still feels the same loyalty to you. It was very sloppy of you allowing yourself to get captured like this."

"You haven't captured me Molek. I'm just deciding whether you are useful enough to keep alive. Do you have a use these days?"

"Brave words from someone who could just about make flowers grow."

"I've changed. And I presume that wherever that portal comes out it will be raining, which means that lightning should not be too hard to channel."

"So, that's it. You want to go home. Well, that portal will be no use to you, it comes out in a military outpost, you'd be killed on sight."

"If that were the case then I doubt you'd tell me, unless you are actually as stupid as you look."

"Is that a chance that you are willing to take?"

"Not at the moment. Ben, would you tie him up please."

“Ben, you come near me and I’ll cosh you again. That is not how today is going to go Yfrey.”

“Perhaps I didn’t make myself clear. You can be tied up and come with us as our prisoner, or, I will just kill you now. Those are your choices.”

“So I am just supposed to submit to you because you claim to have some new power? You don’t actually think I’m that stupid do you?”

With that final statement he swung at her with the cosh. Deftly she dodged to one side and directed a low voltage bolt of lightning from the portal at his feet. A spark landed on his whiskey soaked hassock, which went up in flames. Ben moved surprisingly quickly given his size and physical condition, grabbed the fire extinguisher from the wall and put the fire out. Father Frederick looked shaken but was not seriously injured. Yfrey had only meant to startle him into submission, but she knew that it was important not to show weakness here so attempted to be calm and reserved.

“Was that enough of a demonstration for you?”

“Thank you, Ben. You see now what I mean when I say she’s evil. We righteous men must unite to defeat such abominations.”

“Ben, I don’t have time for you to have a crisis – I need to get Jacques to a healer. You can either help me or I’ll tie you back up again, but neither of you will stop me.”

“Father, Jacques has been shot. Evie knows where she is, I must help her and we should get you to a hospital.”

“Ben, you should be more concerned with your sister’s soul right now, the more time she spends in the company of this evil witch, the less of her there will be left to save. Together we can take her.”

“Sorry Father, I can’t.” Ben hit Father Frederick over the head with the fire extinguisher that he was still holding, knocking him unconscious. “Come on, we can tie him up and put him in the boot of my car. We can drop him at a hospital once Jacques is safe.”

“You know; I didn’t think you had it in you.”

“Nor did I.”

* * *

They dragged the unconscious Molek up the stairs and out through the church. Although it was open for worshippers twenty-four-hours, there was no-one there at what was now four o’clock in the morning.

“We need to get him to a hospital,” Ben persisted as Yfrey helped him heave the dead weight into the boot of his car.

“We need to get to Jacques first. We need as much of a head start as we can get. He’ll come after us as soon as he’s able.”

“That will be a while.”

“Maybe.”

Ben’s hands shook as he fumbled trying to get the key into the ignition. He scratched at the slot but seemed unable to complete the task he had accomplished innumerable times before. Dropping the keys at his feet he smacked the top of the steering wheel in utter frustration.

“Dammit!”

“Ben,” Yfrey touched his arm gently as she stooped, picked up the keys and slotted them into the ignition. “I need you to keep it together, you’re no use to me if you fall apart.”

“What does that mean? Are you going to set me on fire too?”

“Of course not, but this is war and there are going to be casualties.” She hated how much like her brother she sounded.

“And you had to involve Jacques in your war? She isn’t strong enough for this Evie, why have you involved us in your evil war?”

“I did not involve you. I am not the one who attacked Jacques in her place of work or in her home. It was not me who sent an inquisitor to spy on you. They did that. You throw around words like good and evil but do you even know what they mean? I am here to protect you and I’m doing my best. You want out, fine. You can help me get Jacques then you can go back to your self-righteous little world and be content in your own ignorance.”

Ben looked at her, then silently turned the key in the ignition and started to drive.

Chapter Fifteen

Jacques woke up in a cold sweat. Her fever must have broken in the night and for a moment she was disorientated, wondering where she was. Sitting up she went to rub her eyes and the pain in her shoulder reminded her of what had happened. Pulling the chord on the lamp next to her bed revealed Torius sitting on the wicker chair at the bottom of the room, looking at her.

"Welcome back, I thought you might be dying."

"What do you want, Paul?"

"Your knife of course. That's what I wanted before, that's what I want now. You may as well just give it to me, you're in no position to fight."

"How did you get in here?"

"What do you mean? This is my room. I must have made quite an impression when checking in. Yfrey has never been very charismatic, you must have had quite the effect on her."

"You don't know her at all. You've created an image of how you imagine your sister to be, and you've made it real. My brother does the same to me, but he has never tried to kill any of my friends so I guess I have one up on poor Evie."

"You don't have any friends. I know you. That's why you accepted Yfrey so quickly. You are desperate for validation."

"Maybe so, but I don't think I'm the only one. Where are your legions of followers now?"

"Enough! Give me the damn knife so I don't have to hurt you."

"You want to know what I think? I think you need me to give you the knife. Something to do with its magic means that it won't work for you if you simply take it."

"Are you prepared to bet your life on that?"

"I think I am."

"I'm not. You get out of that chair and I will kill you myself." Yfrey stood in the doorway. With the light from the hallway behind her she formed a dark silhouette and threw a long shadow that fell protectively over the bed.

"Yfrey, can't you see that I am trying to save our world?"

"No, you aren't. You are trying to get your own personal glory. If you could see beyond your own ego you would realise that she is the Roghnaithe. We need to protect her. Help me, I don't want to be fighting with you, you're my brother, that has to mean something."

"Yfrey, I…"

Just then Ben stumbled, wheezing and panting into the doorway, knocking Yfrey forward into the room.

"The lifts were out of order." Yfrey explained, never taking her eyes off her brother.

"Jacques…" Ben panted. "She set Father Frederick on fire, with lightning!"

"You lit up a priest?"

"He wasn't really a priest!" Yfrey rolled her eyes in exasperation. "He was an inquisitor, and I didn't mean to set him on fire, just to scare him. He had some sort of fuel on his clothes."

"Did you kill him?"

"No, he's in the boot of the car."

"Of course he is."

"Wait!" Torius jumped to his feet urgently, interrupting the discourse. Immediately Yfrey moved to put herself between him and Jacques. "Who told you the lift was out of order?"

"No-one," Yfrey said suspiciously, eyeing her brother, trying to determine his agenda. "There was a sign on the doors."

"Where was the receptionist?"

"No-one was there."

"We need to move now." His voice was urgent.

"Why?"

"Why would they not want you using the lift?"

"Because it's out of order?"

"Idiot!" Torius shoved Yfrey out of the way, hurried into the hall and pushed the call lift button. By the time everyone else had arrived in the corridor to join him he was already holding the door to the lift open, revealing a trembling receptionist, bound and gagged next to a large black sports bag. "How much do you wanna bet that she isn't heading for the gym? We need to move." He released the door and went to leave.

Jacques caught it and kept it open. "Not without her, pick her up."

"What?"

"When did you stop being a person?" Yfrey demanded angrily. "Pick her up!"

Torius rolled his eyes, grabbed the woman by her bound wrists and slung her over his shoulder as though she was nothing. Ben smashed the fire alarm with his elbow.

"OK, let's move, quickly." Yfrey took Jacques' hand and started to run. Sleepy looking people were already peering out of the doors of their rooms, trying to determine whether the alarm was in fact genuine or if they could just go back to sleep. Ben spoke to each person as he passed them and knocked on unopened doors, trying to explain the urgency of the situation to the unwilling masses.

Outside in the car-park Torius dropped the woman he was carrying on some grass and strode away to Ben's car. Jacques ungagged her and cut her bond using her knife. By now the reluctant evacuees were starting to mill around the assembly point at the back of the car-park, muttering discontentedly about being forced to stir from their beds at this anti-social hour.

"He seemed so nice when the two of you checked in." The woman was watching Torius' back as he strode away. "It's like he's a different person."

"He's nice when it's convenient for him." Jacques too watched him. She wanted him as far away as possible. "You should get to a safe distance with the others if you can walk."

"I need to be the first point of contact for the fire engines. They are automatically alerted when the alarm goes off."

"Right." Jacques tried to sound casual but she wanted to be as far away as possible before any form of authority arrived. She looked around. Yfrey was at the back of the car-park, clearly having some sort of argument with Torius, but there was no sign of Ben.

"Evie!" she called, panicking slightly. "Have you seen Ben?"

Just as she finished her sentence the ground shook and she fell forward onto the grass. Using her good arm she forced herself over onto her back to face the burning building. In what seemed like an instant Yfrey was at her side.

"We have to go now," she said urgently.

"Did you see Ben come out?"

"No, I didn't, but I wasn't looking for him."

"I thought he was right behind us."

"I don't know, I'm sorry."

"I have to find him." Jacques struggled to her feet and stumbled towards the blaze. Yfrey went to say something, but stopped herself, instead following her in silence. They came upon Torius heading away from the flames.

"What are you doing?" he demanded. "We need to get away from here."

"Since when have we been 'we'?" Jacques retorted angrily. Despite her exhaustion she was still a force to be reckoned with. "I need to find my brother. He's never abandoned me and I won't abandon him." This final remark was pointed.

"Your brother's dead, we have to move."

"What? Where is he?" Jacques heard his words but could not absorb them.

"We don't have time for this…" Torius began.

"Show her where the body is." Yfrey cut him off. Her tone told him not to argue.

"Over here, I put the body of the inquisitor next to him. I figured they were both burnt, so it wouldn't look out of place."

"Molek died? We were going to take him to hospital."

"He died after I cut off his airway."

"Why? He didn't need to die, he was beaten."

"As long as he was alive he was a threat. You couldn't do it, so I did. I'll be the villain of this piece as long as you need me to, but I'll keep you alive, I promise you that."

Their conversation was interrupted by a cry from Jacques.

"Ben! No!" She collapsed on her knees next to the body of her brother and shook his shoulders hard. "Ben, wake up! Wake up!" She turned her head to and listened to see if he was breathing. He was not. Her next thought was to attempt CPR. She tried to open his mouth but his lips were burnt shut. "No…" she trailed off in tears. Sitting on the ground next to him she took his hand and began to rock. "No, no, no, no, no, no, no, no…"

"That's the Roghnaithe?" Torius scoffed.

"Do not say another word. You do not know what it is to lose a brother." Yfrey stormed away from him. For the first time he felt shame. He knew he had left her and not given a thought to her wellbeing, but he had not considered how she might feel about losing him.

Gently putting her hand on Jacques' shoulder she spoke softly.

"Come on, we can't help him, we need to move."

"No, no, no, no, no, no, no, no, no…."

"Jacques, come on."

"No, no, no, no, no, no, no, no, no…"

"The sirens are nearly here," Torius approached urgently.

"She's gone; I can't get through." Yfrey looked hopelessly at her brother. "All I had to do was protect her and I failed. I knew I couldn't be the Conduit, but when I met her I started to believe."

"We can protect her together." Torius picked Jacques up as though she weighed nothing and moved quickly towards his car, which he had located earlier in the evening and parked nearby. "Where are we going?" he asked as he laid Jacques on the back seat.

"We need to go home; I know someone who can help us."

"You found a portal?"

"Yes, I did."

"Alright then, let's go."

Chapter Sixteen

Torius carried Jacques through the woods. She was still totally unresponsive. The rain still beat down hard on the travellers; their world had not relented in their absence.

"God, I'd forgotten how damned awful the weather is here." Torius grumbled as his feet sunk into the boggy forest ground. "It's a wonder anyone wants to do anything."

"Well, at least there's a reason I still don't have a clue what I'm doing." Yfrey spoke absentmindedly as she moved lightly between the trees, staying ahead of her brother and plotting a route.

"What does that mean?"

"Something Wrance said. When the rain stops it will all be clear."

"You've seen Wrance? Still spouting prophetic nonsense then. I can't believe you listen to that. How is the old goat?"

"Dead."

"Ah."

"I cut him down from where he hung and he told me that before he died."

"They will pay Yfrey, I will make them pay."

"They are dead too. I lost my temper."

"You killed soldiers?"

"I'm not proud of it."

"I'm proud of you. But they were just soldiers, following orders. We need to cut off the serpent's head."

"That is such rubbish! Just following orders. If those men did not follow orders, then Calim would have no power at all. He'd just be one lonely man shouting insanity into the darkness. His followers are as responsible as he. More so, as the blood is on their hands."

"They would be killed if they didn't obey."

"Only if someone obeyed the order to kill them. Calim has not once bloodied his hands since taking power; he has minions for that."

"I never really thought…"

"No, and if you don't believe in prophecy then why have you been so desperate to get Jacques' knife? Surely one blade is much like another?"

"The blade has mystical qualities. When I disappeared I was tracking a soldier encampment. They had wizards who were trying to determine the source of Calim's downfall and prevent it. They talked about a blade which some mystics had transported to another reality for safe keeping. The General sent assassins after the blade and the woman who was destined to wield it. I wanted to get to it first."

"To wield it yourself?"

"Yes."

"Not everything is about glory Torius. There is a greater good. If you had worked with us instead of against us, then Ben would still be alive and Jacques would still be functioning."

"Ben would have only slowed us down."

"We would not have brought him here. He didn't need to die, he was a good man."

"He was weak."

"We're here. The cottage just there."

She indicated Portan's cottage across the clearing. He had replaced the chickens and acquired a goat, all of which were cowering pathetically from the rain under a makeshift shelter.

"Be careful, there's barbed wire." Yfrey said, remembering her first encounter with the chickens.

"I'm not blind." Torius retorted, stepping over the low fence.

Lightly, Yfrey tapped on the door and waited for a response.

"Who knocks?" a cautious voice came from behind the door.

"A friend."

The door flung open and Portan threw his arms around Yfrey and held her close.

"Yfrey! I felt certain they had killed you! How on Earth did you escape?"

"It takes more than a few pathetic foot soldiers to kill me, but my friend has been shot, can you help her?"

"Of course, come in at once." He stepped to one side to allow them to enter.

"This is my brother, Torius."

"The famous rebel?"

"I see my reputation precedes me." Torius spoke smugly.

"Rebellion can be more dangerous than the most crippling regime if not properly planned," Portan retorted. "Put her in that chair."

"Thank you for doing this. I know we're putting you in danger by being here."

"No-where is safe for a man like me. My only protection is that they are killing the more active people first. They'll come for me eventually. I can sit down and wait or I can do my small part, help you and hope to make a positive change."

"You're a good man."

"No, I'm not. I just don't want to be a victim anymore." He gave her a half smile. "You can go up and change out of your wet things, you know where everything is."

"Come on," Yfrey said to Torius, who looked very out of place in his shirt, jeans and mud caked shoes. "I'll show you where you can put your clothes to dry."

Yfrey had laid her clothes over the heater in what used to be her bedroom and made herself a makeshift dress from the blanket that covered the bed.

"How is she?" she asked Portan as she entered the main room. Jacques was still sitting in the chair, her feet raised on a stool and a blanket covering her. Portan had clearly given her some of his sleeping potion as she was silent and still.

"I have applied the poultice to her wound. It should heal quickly," he said, handing her a bowl of stew. "Your field dressing was excellent; you did half my work for me. Physically she will make a full recovery."

"Her brother died."

"Then she will need time. The mind needs longer to heal than the body."

Just then Torius came downstairs. He cut a comical figure, having borrowed some of Portan's clothes. He was a good three inches taller than the old man and the ill-fitting outfit made him look like a child who was experiencing a growth spurt.

"Do not say a word," he warned Yfrey as she raised her eyebrows quizzically.

"Stew?" Portan offered him a bowl which he took and ate in silence.

"We'll need to take shifts guarding her." Yfrey said after the meal. "She's totally defenceless at the moment and she's all we've got."

"We've got each other."

"She's important. Please."

"Oh, very well. I'll take the first shift if you want."

"Thank you."

Yfrey drew all the curtains and checked that the doors and windows were bolted before going to rest.

"I'll only be a few hours, then we can swap," she promised.

"Just get some sleep. I'll sleep when you wake up. We need to be at our best, not half functioning."

"Are you sure you don't mind?"

"I wouldn't have said so if I did. When did I ever care about hurting your feelings?"

"That is true."

"Well then, get some sleep."

"Torius?"

"What?"

"Thank you."

"You're welcome."

"Torius?"

"WHAT?!"

"I'm glad you're back."

"Whatever."

"Good night."

"Get lost!"

* * *

Portan was waiting for Yfrey at the top of the stairs holding an oil lamp.

"Hi. Thanks for taking us in."

“You are always welcome here Yfrey, you know that.”
“Still, I want you to know we’re grateful.”
“I know that,” he hesitated. “Yfrey?”
“Yes?”
“Is she… the Roghnaithe?”
“I believe she is.”
“Then the prophecies are true.”
“Yes.”
“All of them?”
“I like to think that our prior knowledge means that we can affect the outcome.”
“But what if you can’t?”
“I can’t think like that now. As long as he’s here, with us, he’s safe.”
“I understand, but what if…”
“I can’t do this now.”
“I understand. Good night.”
“Good night.”
She moved silently down the landing until she reached her room. It felt warm and familiar. She lay down and rested her head on the pillow. She wanted to think, but she was so utterly exhausted that she fell fast asleep.

Part Two: The Seer Chronicle

Chapter Seventeen

The wizard, Corsah was afraid. Until now he had been of use to his master. His ability to look in upon the lives of others had made him an invaluable asset, but now he saw nothing. A spellbinder with no powers was of no purpose, and he feared that he had made himself expendable. He fumbled around his work bench, increasing the amount of herbs he usually used in his sight potion and feeding the fire beneath the cauldron, hoping that the added heat would somehow remedy the immediate problem. The mixture boiled, and he saw it bubble, but nothing else. The door slammed shut, causing him to start.

"What ho, Wizard, is there news of Kemp?" Calim was before him. He had the sort of gentle face and quiet manner that could deceive a person unacquainted with him that he was a reasonable man. His gentle green eyes looked questioningly at Corsah, who focused his gaze on his master's neatly kept red beard rather than make eye contact.

"I have lost sight of both Kemp and Molek, My Lord. I don't know what could have happened."

"Have you lost sight, or is there nothing to see?"

"My Lord?"

"You can't see the dead, can you?"

"No, My Lord, but the world they were in was ignorant of our kind, and their laws favour incarceration over execution. Had they been captured I would see them imprisoned."

"Did you, or did you not tell me that the rebel Torius had fled to that world?"

“Why, yes My Lord, but he integrated himself and began to exist as one of them. He was a coward, who ran away. Kemp told me he was no longer of interest to the government.”

“And now Kemp is gone from your vision; I think it may be time to accept the possibility that the good general was incorrect in this instance. So, what are you waiting for?”

“My Lord?”

“Show me Torius!”

“Yes, My Lord, of course, I’m sorry.”

Silently Corsah prayed that he had not lost his power of sight as he mumbled the words to the Revealing spell. Surely enough, the bubbling stopped and the liquid rippled from the middle outwards, until the clouded waters cleared to reveal an image of Torius. The two men peered into the cauldron to see what their quarry was doing.

* * *

Yfrey had not informed Torius about the prophecy of his death. She knew that he would simply brush it off as nonsense and continue to be as cavalier as ever; the exercise had seemed futile. Instead, she and Portan had devised a plan whereby he did not leave the cottage alone. Yfrey had managed to convince him that he was the only one strong enough to protect Jacques, and requested that he stay with her at all times. He had not taken much convincing. His need to be a hero was as strong as ever and his assuredness in his own superiority made him an easy mark in schemes such as this.

This situation was becoming increasingly volatile, however. Since Jacques had regained consciousness she had been extremely hostile. Yfrey was met with icy politeness, but Torius was treated with utter hatred. It was clear that she had decided they were responsible for the death of her brother. She stayed only because she was still weak, and really had nowhere else to go.

It was another dull day and the rain beat mercilessly at the window. Jacques was sitting staring into the fire and Torius was pacing up and down the side of the room, like a caged animal.

“I was wondering if you would like me to teach you Boxcha?” Portan said pleasantly, sitting himself in the chair opposite Jacques and pulling a small round table between them.

“What is it?” Jacques responded dully, never taking her eyes off the flames.

“A child’s game!” Torius snorted derisively as he continued to pace, watching the rain.

“It’s a game of strategy,” Portan continued calmly, choosing to ignore this comment.

“What does it involve?” Jacques asked, turning to face him. She was grateful to the old man for helping her and taking her in. He was the only one in the house who received a kind word from her.

“Well, both players have an area of the board to defend and a limited number of pieces with which to do so. The objective is to take over your opponent’s section of the board whilst defending your own. Different pieces are used in different ways and have different strengths and the winner is the one to successfully utilise each piece to its best advantage and take the board.”

“You’ll have to teach me as we go.”

“Perhaps you could watch Torius and me play, and I could talk you through each move as I make it.”

“Oh fine, prepare to be defeated old man!” Torius laughed triumphantly at the prospect of his certain victory and pulled up a stool to the small table. Jacques glared at him but did not say anything.

“These smaller pieces are called foot soldiers,” Portan explained as he set up the three-tiered board.

“You get more of them, so they are perhaps more expendable than your larger, more powerful pieces. But be careful, without them your more important pieces become vulnerable. This piece is your wizard. It can move anywhere on the board, but has no power. If you are able to move it next to a foot soldier, then you can promote that foot soldier to a king or a destroyer. If you move it next to an opponent’s piece, then that piece can be demoted to foot soldier. The destroyers can destroy up to three pieces before they have to leave the game and can only move two squares per turn. The king is your most powerful piece. If it shares a square with an opponent’s piece, then that piece is automatically removed from the board and cannot be replaced. It can move anywhere on the board. You can have as many kings as you can make, but you start with just one and if all your kings are taken then the game is forfeit. You can watch us to pick up the rest of it."

The game began. Torius clearly favoured his king, leaving his other pieces in their starting positions as he moved it around, eliminating Portan's pieces from the board. Portan avoided the thrusts of the king as best he could whilst moving his pieces to surround Torius' base. It was not long before it was taken.

"Your flaw is that you favour your strongest piece over your other, weaker ones. Sometimes strength is best found in unity." Portan offered by way of advice.

"Whatever. Let's see her do better."

"You are such an arse!" Jacques exploded. "For once in your life take some advice! I could see you were going to lose as soon as you started playing with just one piece. It doesn't matter how strong your piece is, against an army it won't win!"

"You so clever let's see you beat me! Set them up old man!"

Portan smiled quietly to himself as he set up the pieces. Now he would see if his theory was correct.

Torius again led with his king. Jacques' strategy was different from Portan's. Rather than sacrificing any piece she built a defensive line to block his attacks. Her aim was not to destroy his pieces, but to assimilate them. Using her wizard she turned each piece to her colour until the only piece he had left on the board was his king.

"You've lost." Jacques said flatly.

"You cheated."

"Yes, I suppose using my brain was unfair of me since you seem to have left yours somewhere."

"Who the hell do you think you are?"

"I know who I am. I'm not the one kidding myself that I'm some sort of hero."

"If I hadn't promised Yfrey I would teach you to mind your mouth!"

"Well, she's not here, go on, teach me." Jacques stood up and pushed her chair out of the way. "I'm fairly certain that beating the shit out of you will make me feel a whole lot better."

“I don’t need this, I’m going out!”

“No! You need to stay here!” Portan stood up and grabbed his arm.

“Get off me!” Torius punched Portan in the face sending him reeling to the ground. He stormed out into the rain.

* * *

“Where is he going?” Calim demanded.

“He seems to be heading to Sráidbhaile,” Corsah spoke nervously.

“Excellent. I will send word to General Verm to retrieve him; he has a special interest in this case. A public trial and execution is just what we need to squash these murmurings of discontent I’ve been hearing about. It’ll cheer me up too.” As he left the work room he turned again. “Good job.”

“Thank you, My Lord.” Corsah felt a strange combination of relief and guilt. He hated his life

Chapter Eighteen

Yfrey came running down the stairs at the sound of the argument. Jacques was kneeling over Portan, who was lying on the floor, bleeding from his lip. She pressed a handkerchief to his mouth.

"What happened?"

"Your bastard brother happened! Punched him in the mouth."

"Oh, no! Portan, are you alright?"

"I'll be fine; it looks worse than it is. He's got a temper."

"He needs someone to put him in his place," Jacques said angrily, as she helped Portan up and into a chair.

"Where is he now?" Yfrey asked.

"He left," Portan said, dabbing his lip. "You should go after him."

"Why? Good riddance!" Jacques snorted.

"I'll leave him to cool off, he'll be fine."

"Yfrey, have you forgotten what day it is?"

"Oh no!"

"What?" Jacques demanded, forgetting for the moment that currently she did not like Yfrey very much.

"Today is the day he is destined to die. I thought I could prevent it by keeping him here, but prophecies have a way of fighting back." As she spoke, she pulled her coat on and tucked her knife into her belt. "I need to go after him."

"Not on your own." Jacques too pulled on her coat. Her knife was always with her.

"You're not well enough."

"I'm fine." They looked at each other for a moment. "This doesn't make us friends."

"Understood."

Yfrey tracked her brother the same way she had tracked Wrance, what now seemed like an eternity ago. The trail was still fresh and it was an easier hunt. They closed in on the outskirts of a village and she signalled Jacques to stop. On a podium in the centre of a large group of people stood a big, muscular man, dressed in black leather. He carried a mace. Next to him, hands bound and head hanging low, was a severely beaten Torius. Guards stood around the edge of the platform holding guns. Their presence was clearly designed to prevent any rescue attempt, although the crowd was far too passive to make that seem likely.

"They would have bloody guns, wouldn't they?" Jacques muttered.

"If we can get the crowd out of the way I can bury the guards," Yfrey whispered back. "The guy on the platform might be a problem, I can't bury him without sending Torius with him."

"OK, I'll take him. How tough can he be if he needs a mace?"

Yfrey was not really sure how to answer that, but the question seemed to be rhetorical anyway.

"I will show you what we do to traitors!" the man was saying loudly, raising his mace.

"Wait!" Jacques spoke loudly, stepping into view. "I can't see! How can I learn anything if I can't see? Excuse me please, can I get to the front? Excuse me." The confused crowd dispersed as she made her way through. The guards drew their weapons and pointed them at her. "That's OK," she said when the people were out of the way, "carry on." As she spoke she felt the ground tremble beneath her. She knew Yfrey was working her magic, so she leapt onto the podium, knocking Torius on his rear as she landed.

"What the hell are you doing?" General Verm demanded.

"I'm a mace groupie, can I touch your mace?"

"Certainly." He swung it hard at her head. She ducked and in an instant her knife was in her hand. It seemed to sing as she moved with it rhythmically, and her deft movements seemed almost dance-like. She avoided the swinging mace and even dealt a few blows of her own, shallow sweeping cuts, rather than risk losing her weapon in a deep stab. Finally, she was knocked from her feet and Verm delivered what he thought was the death-blow. Jacques rolled out of the way and the mace was stuck in the wooden platform. She kicked sharply at his lower legs, knocking them out from under him. As he fell from the platform, Verm hit his head on the edge of it, landing unconscious on the ground. Jacques moved quickly to cut Torius' bonds. As she did so she noticed the warmth of the sun on her face. The rain had stopped. Yfrey moved through the crowd to the platform and climbed up. She knew what to do.

"People," she spoke loudly and clearly. "Calim has had us living in fear for too long. I have travelled to other worlds and seen that things do not have to be this way. Ever since he seized control, Calim has kept us at war. We just haven't been fighting back. This is The Roghnaithe. Her coming signals that the time is here to fight back. If we want change then we have to make it happen! Stand with us!"

Suddenly the crowd began to cheer. This was unexpected. Yfrey did not know what she expected the result of her speech to be, but it certainly wasn't cheering.

"Evie," Jacques spoke quietly next to her. "I can't protect all these people."

"They don't need you to protect them; they need you to lead them."

At that moment, Verm began to stir on the ground. The crowd fell silent, waiting to see what would happen next. Jacques heaved the mace from its position wedged in the platform and pointed it at Verm.

"You go back to your master and you tell him that he is now at war. You tell him that this is the first in many victories and soon he will fall. You tell him that it is written that The Roghnaithe will be his downfall and I am here to make it so. Go, now." As Verm struggled to his feet she leaned into Yfrey and whispered "That is written, right?"

"Yes, it is." Yfrey lightly touched her friend's arm. The people of the village were milling around excitedly, awaiting instructions. Jacques knew she had to come up with something to say. She had started this thing; these people were now her responsibility.

Corsah looked down on the scene that was playing out in his cauldron. He felt a sinking feeling in the pit of his stomach.

"Oh dear, Calim is not going to like this, not at all."

Chapter Nineteen

"We need to go somewhere safe." Jacques said firmly as she, Yfrey and Torius all sat in conference in what appeared to pass for a pub in this strange world. The table was solid wood, as were the benches on which they were seated. There was no specific bar area and drinks appeared to be poured directly from barrels. As far as she could tell there was no specific system in place for paying for drinks, although the owner of the strange tavern had insisted on keeping their glasses filled free of charge.

"We aren't going to hide like cowards!" Torius said firmly, clearly undaunted by his recent ordeal.

"New rule," Jacques said without looking at him. "You are no longer allowed to speak unless you can first convince both Evie and me that what you are about to say is not profoundly stupid."

"Being brave is no good if you're dead." Yfrey added.

"I'm so glad you two are friends again." Torius said ironically.

"We aren't friends," Yfrey said a little sadly. "We are just both able to identify when you are being an idiot, which isn't hard as it seems to be most of the time."

"We are friends," Jacques said, taking her hand and smiling weakly. "I don't blame you for Ben," she turned to Torius. "I blame you. If it weren't for you none of this would have happened. I will not allow you to put us, or any of these people in danger. If I have to put you down myself then I will. And you know I can."

Torius looked down and did not speak again.

"When that vision in leather returns to his king, he will tell him exactly what happened. I am willing to bet he will rain merry hell down on this village to make an example of it. We need to get these people somewhere safe."

"I'm not the one you have to worry about."

Jacques drew her blade and rose quickly at the sound of Verm's voice behind her.

"Did I not almost kill you enough?" she demanded.

"Easy Roghnaithe, I came to talk, not fight." He raised his arms to show that he was unarmed.

"Sit down and keep your hands on the table," Jacques instructed.

"What do you want?" Yfrey asked suspiciously.

"I want to join you," Verm said, keeping both hands firmly on the table. "I can't go back to Calim and report this failure. If he lets me live he will send me back with men to massacre this village. I'm a soldier, not a butcher. I joined the army to protect the helpless people of this land, not crush them under my boot."

"You had no problem crushing me," Torius snorted.

"You are an arrogant pillock. I still have no problem crushing you." Verm kept his eyes on Jacques as he spoke.

"Man has a point," Jacques added. "I have no problem crushing you either."

"Don't." Yfrey said firmly before Torius could retort. "That's a very nice speech, but how do we know we can trust you?"

"My allegiance change is already known, Calim will have word spread throughout the battalions to have me killed on sight now. If you reject me I am on my own."

"How?"

"He has a wizard, a seer. I am certain that he will have wanted to gloat over the death of this one. He will have seen his plan has failed."

"What traitor would work for Calim?" Torius demanded angrily.

"His name is Corsah, and like most of us he is weak and afraid," he turned to Jacques. "What you did today gave me, as well as the village hope. He will want to kill you for that."

"I can cast a spell to cloud his vision," Yfrey said thoughtfully. "But he will be able to break through it eventually. We need a permanent solution."

"I can get you close," Verm said. "I know the road to Central City well and I still have friends there, although I haven't been back in years." He studied Yfrey's face with interest. "I can't guarantee it's a mission we'd come back from."

"I understand. I'll cast the spell to cloak Jacques and Torius first. They can work on training the resistance, then if we don't return they will be prepared."

"Evie, no!" Jacques grabbed her wrist firmly. "You can't just go on a suicide mission, especially with someone who wanted to kill us not very long ago."

"I have no intention of dying, but we're at war, we must form alliances where we can."

"We should get back to Portan, make sure he's safe, then you can cast your spell."

"We must bring these people with us, he's in the middle of the forest, it will be easier to fortify."

"I can help with the fortifications; I've done it before. And I can help you train the soldiers if you want me to." Torius offered.

"Fine, but first you are going to apologise for hitting him, or you can sleep in a tree." Jacques said firmly.

"Yes." Yfrey said, suddenly remembering what her brother had done. "That old man is under my protection, you never touch him again."

"I'm sorry," Torius had nothing else to say.

"Alright, we should get all the people from this village who are prepared to come with us and move, now. It's not safe here any more." She turned to Verm, "You should go with Evie to our friend. He's a healer and can treat your wounds. You'll be no use to anyone if you're dead." Verm nodded.

"What are you going to do?" Yfrey asked uncertainly.

"I'll stay here and rally the troops, so to speak. I need to work out what we're dealing with."

"Alright, be careful."

"Always am."

Yfrey still did not trust Verm as she led him through the woods to Portan's cottage. She trusted Jacques and knew that if she was going to grow as a leader, then she could not second guess all her decisions. So, she did not speak of her suspicions, instead leading the way in silence.

"What on earth made you so powerful?" Verm asked conversationally, clearly uncomfortable with the silence of their journey. "I always thought you people were peaceful."

"Necessity." Yfrey did not look at him as she replied. "We aren't all so easily stamped by people like you, obeying orders."

"Obeying orders is just an excuse for not taking responsibility for your actions," Verm spoke seriously. "I joined the army to protect people, and make a difference."

"What difference would killing my brother have made?"

"Well, for one thing it would have made me feel a hell of a lot better."

"Why?"

"When Calim came to power, my unit and I were on a routine patrol of the border lands. I had watched him campaign and did not like his ideas. On a number of occasions, I had spoken out against him. Within three months, we received the message that we were being recalled for debriefing. I had intended to resign my commission and retire somewhere quiet as soon as my term was up. When we returned, Calim sent for me. I felt certain that he was going to have me arrested for dissident behaviour. But instead he wanted to inform me of the death of my father at the hands of a raiding party led by your brother."

"What?" For the first time Yfrey looked at him. He had a strong square jaw, which was made to look more so by a well trimmed beard framing his face. A scar ran down the entire left side of his face, from forehead to jowl and distorted his appearance. The mutilation made his left eye seem lower than the right and it did not open as widely. Despite all of this, he no longer looked intimidating to her, just profoundly sad.

"I returned to the village to see for myself," he continued. "There was nothing left."

"I'm sorry," Yfrey touched his arm gently. "My brother is very focused, but he lacks compassion."

"He was a healer, a gentle man. He would never have hurt anyone."

"I'm sorry," Yfrey said again. "We're here; would you stand against the wall? My friend is nervous around soldiers and I'll have to break you to him gently."

Obediently, Verm stood behind the door against the wall, as Yfrey tapped lightly and called, "It's me."

Portan opened the door quickly.

"Yfrey! I am so glad you survived! Jacques?"

"She's fine, she stayed behind. Things are happening more quickly than anticipated. There's someone…" she trailed off as Portan was no longer looking at her, but over her shoulder at Verm who had stepped forward.

"Verm?"

"Father?"

"They told me you had been killed in battle."

"You aren't dead!" Verm rushed forward and grabbed both Portan's upper arms in his hands to ascertain proof of a physical presence. "There was a raid on your village, I saw the carnage!"

"There was, but I was in the forest gathering supplies at the time. When I returned, the inquisitor was already there to investigate. He saw my herbs and arrested me for witchcraft. I kept telling them that I was not a witch, that you were my son, that you'd vouch for me. That's when they told me you'd died."

Verm went very quiet, his expression was black as night.

"He's been hurt," Yfrey spoke to break the silence. "Can you help him?"

"Yes, of course. Come in both of you."

Portan treated Verm's injuries in silence whilst Yfrey worked upstairs on a cloaking spell. It was late when she heard Jacques and Torius return. She hurried downstairs to meet them.

"Well?"

"We managed to relocate the entire village into the forest. We have built makeshift shelters and your brother fortified the outskirts with some sort of magic."

"A warning incantation," he clarified.

"We have lookout posts and lots of camouflage."

"I'm going to take some of the more able men out tomorrow to other villages. We need to recruit more members to our ranks." Torius chimed in.

"I'll train those who remain behind in martial arts. They need to be able to defend themselves."

"That's good. Verm and I will leave first thing tomorrow. Calim has had the upper hand too long." Yfrey said.

"Do you have a plan you can show me? I want you to be safe."

"If you come with me to the book, I can project a route of our journey for you?" Yfrey offered.

"That's fine."

When they were alone upstairs, she opened the book and started to make markings in the linen.

"Evie, that's alright, I don't need to see your route. I just wanted to make sure you were alright, you know, with Vern. I think he could be dangerous and I don't want you getting hurt."

"We can trust Verm, he's Portan's son. He has as much reason to want Calim deposed as we do. Are you alright?"

"I don't know. This has all happened so fast. And it's just me. Most days I feel like I'm battling an army, but not a real one! What if I'm not ready?"

Yfrey took both her hands and moved close to her, so their foreheads were almost touching.

"You are ready. You're the strongest person I know. You have power that I can only dream about. You need to learn to channel it, and your knife can help with that. And so can I when I get back. But I have to go, I have to keep you safe, it's my job."

"How about we agree to keep each other safe?"

"We can do that."

Chapter Twenty

It was still dark when Yfrey awoke early the next morning. She moved downstairs quietly, so as not to wake anyone. Verm was already outside, an arsenal of weapons laid out on a sheet on the ground in front of him.

"Morning." He looked up upon hearing her come out. He was in the process of cleaning a pistol.

"You planning a war?"

"We're already at war, I just want to be prepared. There is a battalion camped out not two ricons from here. We can surprise them and take their land craft. With transportation we can be at Central City in three days."

"I can't cloak a land craft. We'd be safer walking."

"Walking would take months! And who knows what kind of dangers we'd encounter? Why can't you cloak land craft?"

"Because they aren't natural. They aren't supposed to be here so they are difficult to conceal."

"What about horses? Can you cloak horses?"

"Yes."

"Then we will take their horses and disable their land craft so they can't follow us." He started to strap the weapons to himself. "Aren't you going to arm yourself?"

"I have my knife."

"That's all?"

"That's all I need."

Verm looked slightly sheepish as he clipped some ammunition into his pistol and holstered it at his waist.

"Alright then, shall we go?"

"Lead the way."

They moved quickly and quietly through the woods. For a large man, Verm moved with surprising stealth and agility. He was solid and powerful and Yfrey knew she would not be victorious in an altercation with him. Still, she was not afraid; there was something about him that she trusted.

"My Father told me what you did for him."

"Almost got him killed?"

"Saved his life." Verm looked at her, his eyes exuding nothing but kindness and gratitude. "He said I must protect you, and I will, with mine. A life for a life."

"You are an honourable man, and I love your father as though he were my own, but you must prioritise your own life; he needs you more than me."

"Quiet… the camp is just through those trees."

They moved quietly to the edge of the forest to get a better view of the encampment. Three horses were tethered to a wooden pole in between some tents. There was one guard, pacing about looking annoyed that he had pulled the night watch.

"Only three horses?" Yfrey whispered as she scanned the camp for a possible tactical advantage.

"Only officers get horses." Verm leaned in close to her ear as he spoke so that she could feel his hot breath of the back of her neck. "It's sort of a status symbol; you ride around inspecting the troops. Some find it a good vantage point from which to kick the ranks. Conduct unbecoming of an officer was no longer relevant when Calim took power."

"Where are the land craft? We should disable them first."

"They'll be around the front of the tents. Follow me."

They crept between the tents until they were so close to the horses that they could smell them.

Crouched down behind some canvas, Yfrey hissed, "We need to wait until that guard is a good distance away. If he raises the alarm we could be in trouble."

"That's Brant." There was a distinct tone of distaste in Verm's voice. "I had him discharged, he's a sadistic bastard. Glad to know my recommendations are taken so seriously."

Just then a strong wind blew through the encampment and startled the horses. One began to whinny and stamp, causing the others to pull at their tethers. Annoyed, Brant picked up a stone and hurled it at the horses.

"Shut up you stupid beasts!" The anger in his voice seemed both hateful and excessive. Before Yfrey knew what was going on, Verm was behind Brant and had him in a choke hold. The man struggled and kicked but was unable to make a sound. Reacting quickly to the change of plans, Yfrey moved to calm the horses. The one the stone had struck was bleeding and lame. She took some clay and coated the wound but she knew it was unrideable. Brant was unconscious and limp in Verm's arms.

"Untie the horses, we'll leave Brant tied to the pole as a replacement," he said.

"This one is too lame to ride," Yfrey said sadly.

"We'll take it back to my father. If we leave it here it will be shot."

"Fine. I'll go and bury the land craft, you prepare the horses, then we go before anyone wakes up."

They rode quickly through the forest, leading the lame colt behind them. Verm was atop a handsome piebald stallion whilst Yfrey rode a beautiful palomino. She used her cloaking abilities to conceal their tracks as they made their way back to Portan's cottage. When they arrived in the clearing Jacques rushed out to meet them.

"Evie! I thought you'd left without saying goodbye."

"No, just needed to pick up a few things," Yfrey lied. She had wanted to leave without saying goodbye. She found goodbyes awkward. "Look, we brought you a present." She indicated the black colt they had been leading as she dismounted.

"You brought me a horse…" Jacques began awkwardly. She did not even like dogs.

"He needs work," Yfrey said as she took Jacques by the hand and led her towards the creature. "The cut on his leg is fresh and Portan will need to treat it. These scars are old," she indicated scarring on the creature's neck and torso. "He may need some help trusting again."

Jacques looked sadly at the horse's scars and then reached out and touched its nose. It leaned in towards her and breathed its steaming breath on her hand.

"He has gentle eyes," she observed. "I will call him Ben."

"He'll look after you while I'm away."

"Don't go. You cast a cloaking spell, won't that be enough until we're ready to fight?"

"I have to go. Corsah will already be working to counteract my spell. As long as he is free to do so, you aren't safe, and I have to protect you."

"Then I should come. I can help. I don't want people risking themselves for me."

"It is more important that you survive than I. You are more than a person; you are a symbol of hope. It was prophesied that you would come and the people will unite behind you. You are giving them something to believe in."

"You know I don't believe in prophecy."

"You don't have to. Just by being here you are a symbol. Work with Torius. He is very charismatic and will help you recruit and train followers; he's done it before. Just don't let him go out on his own, unprepared. He is headstrong and not used to following orders and he could get you in trouble that way."

"I don't trust him Evie."

"Don't trust who?" Torius was suddenly with them. He had a new sword which he had clearly found somewhere and was swinging it around and showing off. Ben started and began to stomp the ground nervously. Yfrey grabbed the reins and tried to calm the creature but it fought her.

"Hey! Would you watch it with that thing?" Jacques was annoyed as she dodged another swing.

Suddenly Torius' sword was flung from his hands and, as he turned to see what happened, he was met with a gloved fist squarely in his face. He landed flat on his rear in the mud.

"Oh, I'm sorry, I thought you were the enemy." Verm said smugly as he offered a hand to Torius, who was now bleeding from the nose. He had emerged from the cottage with Portan, who was applying a poultice to the wounded horse.

“How did you get his sword off him?” Jacques asked, grinning. “That was cool.”

Verm showed her his own weapon. It consisted of two parallel blades which came together in a point at the top.

“I made it myself. If you catch an enemy’s weapon in the gap then it doesn’t take much force to twist if from their grip,” he offered it to Jacques. “You should take it. Something tells me you’ll need it more than I.”

“Thank you.”

“Are you ready?” he said, turning to Yfrey.

“That I am.”

“Evie…”

“I’ll be fine, don’t worry.”

“Well, you’d better be. If I have to come and get you I’ll be cross.”

“Try not to kill my brother.”

“No promises.”

With that Yfrey and Verm mounted their horses and rode away into the forest.

Chapter Twenty-One

Yfrey and Verm rode side by side in relative silence. It was not awkward, more that neither of them had anything to say to the other and felt no particular need to fill the silence with idle chatter. By dusk they were approaching the outskirts of the forest that had provided their cover and protection until now. Verm raised his hand to indicate that they should stop.

"We should wait here until it's completely dark, then we can move through quickly until we can find more cover," Yfrey hissed.

"I was thinking more we could see if we can get a bed for the night," Verm said calmly. "The horses need to rest, and I'm not as comfortable sleeping in mud as you are. Also, I'm hungry."

"We don't know if we can trust these people."

"We don't have to trust them; they don't know who we are. All we have to do is blend in."

"I've never been a big blender. I'm not a people person."

"But you can appear as anyone, right? We've all been briefed on your witchy ways. Make yourself look like a soldier. Trust me, we'll be OK."

"So we're just gonna ride into town?"

"Look like a soldier… wow, that's good, and I'm a little disturbed. We could have met before and I would never know."

"We've never met before."

"Right. And I'm just supposed to believe that. You could be that woman who seduced me and stole my purse. Do you have a birth mark behind your ear?"

"No. You know, if we are going to work together we need to be able to trust each other. The illusion does not withstand close scrutiny. We have been demonised by the authorities. That, 'they could be anywhere' line just leads to the sort of paranoia that saw your father tortured and mutilated."

"I know that. I'm a free thinker, not a drone. I was trying to break the ice by being witty. All those powers and you don't have room for a sense of humour, huh?"

"Ever consider that you just aren't funny?"

"Never." His eyes sparkled as he tethered their horses to a food trough outside an inn. "I don't get all the women I get because of my dashing good looks," he gestured to his scar as they entered the tavern.

"What can I do for you gentlemen?" A large breasted bar maid carrying a tray of drinks acknowledged them as they entered.

"My friend and I would like some food and a room for the night." Verm slapped Yfrey unnecessarily hard between the shoulder blades causing her to step forward and cough.

"Wow, you're strong. What did he do to offend you?" The barmaid was already looking Verm up and down admiring his large biceps and broad shoulders.

"Oh, it's just how men show affection for each other, right kid?" Verm grinned as he slapped Yfrey's behind equally as hard.

"Absolutely, bro," Yfrey replied as she punched him hard in the genitals. Verm doubled over and coughed, his eyes glistened with tears. "All in good fun. Do you have any rooms?"

"You want two rooms?"

"Yes!" They spoke simultaneously.

They seated themselves in the bar area to order food. It was a set up that Jacques would have been more comfortable with than the tavern in the previous village. There was a specific area to order food and drink and pay, and although old fashioned by the standards of her world, there were tables and booths so it would have been much easier to acclimatise to. Still, Jacques was not here; Yfrey was sitting across the table from Verm who seemed determined to draw as much attention to himself as was humanly possible. He flirted shamelessly with every female who came into close enough vicinity of him until Yfrey became quite cross.

"This is not blending in!" she hissed angrily once the barmaid was out of earshot.

"In case you failed to notice, I am six foot seven, broad, with very distinctive facial features and a scar so deep that nothing will hide it. I do not have your ability to appear differently. If it looks like you want attention, then you are less likely to be noticed. And, if I get a bit of tail out of it, then that's a bonus. Man can't live by badly made stew alone," he indicated the food which they had been served with this last comment. It really was terrible. Before Yfrey had a chance to respond the busty barmaid was back and this time she was dragging a friend in her wake.

"We just got off shift," she announced, straddling Verm and indicating that her friend should sit down next to Yfrey. Yfrey nervously huddled into the corner of the booth and smiled weakly at the woman who seemed to be looking to her friend for further instruction.

"Doesn't your friend like girls?" the barmaid demanded as she briefly stopped licking Verm's ear long enough to check on her friend's progress. Yfrey looked like a rabbit caught in the headlights, pressed right up against the wall.

"He's shy," Verm grinned, clearly enjoying how uncomfortable Yfrey was at this moment. "Me," he continued loudly. "I prefer the direct approach. I have a room upstairs, wanna get more direct?"

The barmaid grinned, dismounted and held out her hand to him. Verm winked at Yfrey as he left.

"Don't do anything I wouldn't do."

"I really hate you at the moment."

"Ah, it'll pass; everyone loves me eventually."

When he was gone, the woman sitting next to Yfrey spoke to her for the first time.

"I'm Borana. I'm sorry about my friend, she's pushy. I mean, I could see you weren't interested. Have you got a girl back home?"

"Something like that." Yfrey was relieved that she was not going to have to fend off unwanted advances. She had a feeling that had Verm's conquest wanted her, then things would be very different about now.

"Well, she's lucky to have someone so loyal to her."

"She deserves loyalty."

"I'm staying with Toria, I had some problems with my place. How long do you think they'll be? I have no way of getting into the house without her."

“I wouldn’t guess at more than ten minutes,” Yfrey said dryly.

Borana grinned broadly.

“Well, that gives us time for a drink! Same again for you?”

“Yes, please.” Yfrey smiled as the woman made her way to the bar. This wasn’t so bad. And at least while she was drinking in company she was less conspicuous.

Just then the doors to the tavern flew open and three armed soldiers barged in.

“Who do those horses outside belong to?” one demanded loudly. The bar was silent. “No-one?”

Yfrey kept very quiet. She would not let anyone suffer for her, but she wanted to see how this panned out before making a move.

“Well, whoever it is will be in to collect them so we’ll wait. You’ll keep us company won’t you darling?” He grabbed Borana and pulled her close to him so that their groins were touching.

“I’m here with a friend,” she began awkwardly, trying to wriggle free from his grip.

“Ooo, we’ve got a wriggler! Little to the left sweetheart if you’re going to do that.”

“Hey!” Yfrey had already had enough. “She’s with me.” She stood up and hoped that she appeared as big and tall as she was trying to project.

“Stand down son,” the soldier turned to face Yfrey, keeping Borana in place by holding her hair.

“You don’t know who you’re dealing with.”

“Oh, I think I do. Why don’t we talk about this outside?”

“I like it in here.”

Yfrey drew her knife. She did not have Jacques’ skills as a martial artist or Torius’ strength. She was going to have to bluff her way out of this.

“That’s a witch’s blade, where did you get that?”

“Where do you think?”

“You a hunter?”

“You an idiot?”

"Come here and say that!" The soldier shoved Borana to the floor and squared up to Yfrey.

"You don't want to mess with me."

"Really? Why not?"

"Because he's with me." Verm strode down the stairs. He was only wearing his trousers and his well-defined torso rippled beneath a thick coating of black hair. In his right hand he was gripping his mace.

"General Verm!" All the soldiers stood to attention.

"What the hell is this about?" Verm demanded.

"These idiots had a problem with our horses, then tried to take my woman!" Yfrey did not really know how men spoke to each other and hoped this sounded convincing.

"Why do you want to know about our horses?" Verm kept his gaze firmly on the man he was speaking to, but his peripheral vision was aware of the other two. He was ready to fight if he needed to.

"Those horses were stolen from our barracks today."

"Those horses were requisitioned from your barracks today." Verm corrected him firmly.

"But Sir…"

"What? Since when did I have to answer to you?"

"You have to answer to me, General Verm," an inquisitor had entered the tavern unnoticed. "Go and get your clothes on, I'm not talking to you like that."

"Why the hell is an inquisitor investigating stolen horses?" Verm demanded, still clutching his mace.

"I am here to investigate the allegation that witches frequent this establishment. Please clothe yourself, I find your semi naked body unpleasant to say the least."

"Go on," Yfrey urged, "we won't continue without you."

For the first time the inquisitor looked at Yfrey, who was still clutching her knife.

"You are here for the same reason as me?" he asked, eyeing her suspiciously.

"I'm surprised they sent such a high ranking person as yourself to such a low level establishment. I was in the middle of an investigation when these idiots barged in causing a fuss. Subtlety not their strong suit."

"No. How would you proceed?" The inquisitor continued to eye Yfrey with suspicion.

"Well, I'd send Captain Tactful and his indelicate underlings out to cover the exits now our cover's been blown. Then I'd wait for the general, he's in charge here, not me."

"You heard him!" the inquisitor suddenly seemed convinced. "Get out and cover the exits. I'll talk to the owner."

The soldier dragged Borana by the hair and threw her at Yfrey as he stormed out. Yfrey sheathed her blade and seated herself back down.

"Are you alright?"

"Not really. Are you really a witch hunter?" As she spoke she pushed a strand of hair behind her ear. For a second it seemed bright white before blending in with the rest of the brown. Yfrey smiled. She wasn't the only one who was undercover.

"Don't worry, you're quite safe with me."

"What do you mean?" Far from having the desired effect of being soothing the words seemed to have panicked Borana. "What do you want me to do?"

"Just trust me. Please don't draw attention to yourself."

At that point Verm came striding down the stairs fully clothed and armed.

"I trust you find me more presentable now?" he demanded, making his way confidently towards the inquisitor.

"Yes. What have you learnt here? You can report to me."

"We haven't had the chance to find out anything, your men totally destroyed months of work."

"Did you hear that?" Yfrey leapt to her feet pretending to be startled.

"What?"

"Something outside."

"Go and check," Verm commanded. He understood.

Yfrey moved quietly outside to deal with the soldiers.

"Well, since subtlety is now out of the question, what do you say to a good old fashioned inquisition?"

“I’m not sure how effective that would be with these people,” Verm began awkwardly.

“Oh, you’d be surprised just how effective my techniques can be.” The inquisitor smiled sadistically.

“Very few things surprise me.”

“General!” Yfrey ran in urgently. “The soldiers are gone!”

“Gone? All of them?” the inquisitor demanded.

“Yes, all of them.”

“You’re sure?” Verm asked carefully.

“Certain.” Yfrey dropped her disguise, revealing herself to the inquisitor and the patrons of the tavern.

“Excellent.” Verm swung his mace hard at the head of the inquisitor, sending a crumpled corpse plummeting to the tavern floor.

“Well?” Yfrey asked irritably.

“Well?” Verm asked.

“What did I say?”

“Oh? You’re actually going to make me do this?”

“I am so going to make you do this.”

“You were right; we should not have come into a public place. Happy?”

“Ecstatic.”

“Good. What do we do with him?”

“Do we need a scarecrow?”

“Yfrey?” Borana stood up and looked at her. “You’re Yfrey? I foresaw your coming.”

“You’re a seer?”

“I am. It’s alright everyone; it’s Yfrey. She has come to save us as I foretold.”

Suddenly a veil was lifted from the bar. All the people in it had bright white hair and intense blue eyes.

“All you people are witches?” Verm stared in amazement. “Why didn’t you fight back?”

“They don’t have that kind of power. Almost all our kind have very limited powers, they couldn’t fight an army.” Yfrey explained as she looked around the room.

“That’s because they lack training and discipline, those things can be taught.”

“We can’t take them with us, the more of us there are the harder they’ll be to hide.”

“They can’t stay here, this place is under observation.”

“We’ll send them to Jacques. She can protect and train them.”

“Where do we go?” Borana asked. “We’re ready to do what needs to be done. We’re just waiting for you.”

“I’ll go upstairs and conjure a guiding light,” Yfrey said. “You should all try and get some rest; we’ll need to move out at dawn.”

Chapter Twenty-Two

"Why can't you see my inquisitor?" Calim demanded, slamming his fist down hard on the table. His usual calm demeanour was distinctly rattled and there was a fury in his eyes which was truly terrifying.

"I'm sorry, My Lord. As soon as they entered that tavern they vanished. I can no longer see the seer you sent them to retrieve either. It's like I've been blinded." Corsah was trembling with fear, if he had outlived his usefulness he would soon know.

"Torius must be blocking you somehow." Calim turned from the table and ran his fingers through his hair. His voice was calm again. He had to think. "He never had that kind of power before. He must be working with someone."

"He was never able to form alliances before." Fosk, who had been sitting in the corner of the room examining his blade, now spoke. "That's why he was never a threat to us; he was just one angry man. If he's now organised, we should end him. Cut off the head of the serpent before it grows."

"I agree." Calim turned to face his second in command. "But how? My seer is defective and we haven't heard from the last battalion we sent to retrieve him. Short of burning down villages until we smoke him out, I'm at a loss."

"Well, that could work." Fosk observed. "People will do almost anything to protect what's theirs. We'd have them falling over themselves to turn him in."

"You could be onto something…"

"With all due respect, My Lord," Corsah interrupted nervously. "Why waste the time and resources?" He swallowed hard as both Calim and Fosk looked enquiringly at him. "I mean," he continued uncertainly, "he has a weakness; his sister. She is low level, limited power. She wouldn't be difficult to capture, then he'd come to us."

"The maggot may be onto something. She was travelling alone the last time we checked. Shouldn't be too hard to capture. The question would be how do we let him know we have her?"

"Well?" Calim turned to Corsah.

"Well, My Lord, we wouldn't have to. We'd just have to make sure her cell is equipped with herbs and other ingredients and she would do it for us."

"Very good!" Calim's eyes lit up. "Go and prepare a room with the appropriate ingredients. Don't make it too obvious. Then take the night off, I'm very pleased with you."

Corsah scuttled away.

"Well, that was productive," Fosk observed. "I should go and see if anyone is stupid enough to be out after Curfew. I hope they are."

"I feel like a blonde tonight. Find me one; I'll be in my room."

"Yes, My Lord."

* * *

The people from the tavern followed the tiny light that Yfrey had conjured. It led them through the dense forests and open fields, but no populated areas. As they came upon a clearing with a small cottage in the middle and some chickens and goats around the outside, they were met by the click of a rifle.

"State your business." The voice was young, barely out of puberty.

"We mean you no harm, we followed the light here." Borana said softly, hoping her tone would calm the youth.

"What light? What are you talking about?" demanded the youth, his tone was agitated.

"Who's in charge here? Let me speak to them."

"I'm in charge." Torius walked over slowly. Reaching over he pushed the watchman's gun out of the way. "It's alright kid, they're with us. Go patrol the perimeter. Did Yfrey send you?"

"Yes, she said we'd be safe from the inquisitors here."

"And so you will. You the leader of this group?"

"We don't really have a leader."

"You do now. Go and report to the cottage. The rest of you can come with me, it's not a free ride here, you'll be expected to work." He led the group away.

Borana made her way tentatively towards the cottage. The door was open and she stepped gingerly over the threshold. Before her she could see an old man, stitching a deep cut on the face of a young woman.

"Oh, I'm sorry…" she began.

"Just a minute," the old man silenced her as he applied the poultice to his finished work and covered it with a cloth. "Alright."

"We done?" Jacques asked, lightly feeling the dressing on her face.

"Yes, you may have a scar but the poultice will minimise visibility."

"Well, I can always cover it with my war paint. Who are you?"

"What happened to your face?" Borana could not help but ask.

"Some soldiers came a bit close to camp. They won't be back, don't worry. Who are you?"

"I'm Borana. Yfrey sent me. She said I'd be safe here."

"She's alright?"

"She's amazing – I've never seen anything like her powers."

"Well, I won't be impressed until she pulls a rabbit out of a hat. Do you have powers?"

"I can see the future. I predicted that she'd come for us."

"You can see the future in an 'oh, that's interesting, I'd better get my will up together' way, or an 'I'd better not do that' sort of a way?"

"Nothing is set in stone. If we know it's coming then it is within our power to change it."

"Excellent. You'll be useful. Take a room upstairs and sort out what you need to see the future. Did you say there were more of you?"

"Yes, the man is setting them up with places."

"Do they all have powers?"

"Most of them."

"Good, I think we'll need that."

"Do you have a plan?" Portan asked as he cleared his medical equipment from the table.

"Not yet, but I will."

Chapter Twenty-Three

"I was thinking," Verm spoke thoughtfully, as he roasted the moonfruit they had foraged over the fire they had set. "Do you believe in destiny?"

Yfrey lowered her hood and looked curiously at him. They were sitting in the forest. Since the incident in the tavern they had avoided populated areas and were camped here for the night. "I mean," he continued, turning the spit absentmindedly. "That woman said she knew you were going to be in the tavern to save her. So, even though it was my stupid idea, and I put us in more danger than was necessary, if it was meant to happen, then I couldn't help it."

"I don't blame you," Yfrey began awkwardly. "We needed to be in that tavern. Helping those people was the right thing to do. But I think we make our own destiny."

"How is it that she saw you then? And what of your Roghnaithe prophecy?"

"I had to believe it to make it happen. Whilst I think there was certainly an element of magic that transported me to the right place and time, I had to be alert to protect us. Things would not have happened on their own. I don't really understand destiny, but I think it's important not to be complacent. When people start to believe that they have no power over their circumstances things start to unravel for them. If you lose faith in yourself then you lose everything."

"You sound like you're speaking from experience." Verm pulled the cooked fruit from the skewer and offered it to her. "When I heard of my father's death I was very angry. My soul became very dark. I blamed the magical community and swore revenge. I think Calim knew what I would do. That's why he told me such a terrible lie. He was the gun and I was the bullet."

"I have done horrible things too. The important thing is that we don't let them define us."

"I arrested people. Witches. Told myself they would get a fair trial. I knew they wouldn't. I am as responsible for the torture and deaths of those people as if I had branded them and strung them up myself. Is there anything in that book of yours about a terrible coward who found redemption?"

"The book's prophecies are vague and open to interpretation. But I don't believe for a moment that you are a coward. You're a person like the rest of us."

"I am nothing like you. You are awesome, driven, a force of good. I've never seen anything quite like you."

"When our village was taken by the soldiers I ran. You've seen what I am capable of, and I ran. My brother always told me I was weak, that I needed him to protect me. Somehow it was easier to believe that. To believe I was helpless. That things were out of my control. If there was nothing I could do but run, then it was easier to live with myself. I could have stopped it if I'd just believed in myself the way my parents and Wrance believed in me. It was just easier to believe that I was helpless."

"Your brother can be very persuasive."

"I know. He claimed that retreat was a tactical manoeuvre to gain the advantage. He launched guerrilla strikes on military bases. He was reckless, but now I realise that he was trying to assuage his guilt over the death of our parents."

"Your brother was reckless; and a poor tactician and leader. He put his men in unnecessary danger for his own glory. He is the most wanted man in the land; he won't win anything with such a high profile."

"When he disappeared I was terrified. All alone, no clue what to do. I lost track of how long I was running. With the rain, days just blended into themselves."

"Well, you've got it together now. You're strong and capable, a force to be reckoned with."

"I've had to be. Jacques needs me strong; I'm no use to her if I fall apart."

"She can handle herself. She beat me good and proper. I'm surprised she didn't kill me."

"She wouldn't. She's not a killer. I'm a killer, I'll carry that burden for both of us."

"Are we going to kill the seer? I mean, it's not a problem, I just want to know what the plan is."

"If we have to kill him then we will. As long as Calim has him then he's a threat. But if there is an alternative then we should take it. I don't just want to kill because it's the simplest solution to a problem."

"Understood. You're a good person, you've had to adapt to very difficult circumstances."

"I'm not making any excuses. I first killed because I was consumed by hate. Now I am prepared to kill to protect Jacques. Different motivation, but it's still disgusting. I'm disgusting, but I do what I must."

"She's lucky to have you…" Verm stopped and raised his hand to silence her. He cocked his head to one side and drew his dagger. Yfrey did the same. In an instant he was attacked from behind. He raised his hand and caught the blow before it made contact with his head. Verm wrenched hard hauling his assailant over his head. The ragged-looking little man landed hard on his back, the wind knocked out of him.

"Who are you and what do you want?" Verm demanded, pressing his knife hard against the man's throat.

"I have no quarrel with you," the man wheezed. "Let us take the witch, we can share the bounty."

"What bounty?" Yfrey moved in closer.

"There is a price on your head, witch! Calim wants you. Apparently your brother has gone too far."

Verm pressed the knife harder but Yfrey stopped him.

"Wait," she said raising her hand. "How did you find us?"

"Magic leaves a taste in the air, and you've been using a lot to cover your trail. Ironic."

"You're a tracker? Why would you turn on your own people?"

"You aren't my people; I don't know you. I need the money."

"And if Calim asks how you found me? You can't tell him the truth, he'll have you branded and condemned. Just leave. Don't come back. I'll kill you if you do."

"Oh, and I'm supposed to believe that you'll just let me walk away?"

"I can barely believe that," Verm said irritably.

"Fine, tie him to a tree. We'll come back for him when the mission is complete."

"Mission?"

"Shut it you." Verm used the hilt of his blade to knock the man unconscious. "OK, once we've tied him up we should move. If there's a bounty on your head, then we can't afford to hang around."

"Agreed."

They bound and gagged the intruder before tying him to a tree and mounting their horses. With a price on her head Yfrey would have to keep moving.

* * *

Jacques wiped the blood from her knife before returning it to her sheath.

"This is your fault." She said, turning to Torius who was sitting in the mud behind her.

"You killed him!" He spoke with utter amazement at the scene which was before him.

"No shit. You can get rid of the body; I've cleaned up enough of your messes lately. Don't leave it there to rot."

"Fine," he grumbled, struggling to his feet. He took one of the corpse's feet and started to drag it out of the clearing. "But I don't see how you killing someone is my fault. I didn't ask you to jump in and help me, I had things under control."

"Oh, yes. You were controlling things beautifully from your seated position in the mud. Sure you had him right where you wanted him. And! It's your fault because there wouldn't be a price on Evie's head if it weren't for you. They think that capturing her will somehow draw you out. Well, I'll tell you this much, if it comes down to you or her then I will hand you over in a heartbeat, do you understand me? There is no choice for me in that instance; I will just give you up."

"You won't have to. I know you don't think much of me, but I love my sister. Everything I've done so far I've done to protect her."

"Rubbish. Everything you've done is for your own personal glory. Evie didn't even fit into the equation."

"Can we do this later please? I'm dragging a corpse here."

"Fine, I'm going in to clean up."

Upon entering the cottage, Jacques was met by Portan, trying to console Borana.

"What happened?" she asked urgently.

"Tell her what you saw, it's important," Portan coaxed.

"Tell me…"

"Yfrey being captured and held in Central Tower. She's in trouble." Borana was clearly traumatised by the vision.

"Has this happened or is it a future event?"

"I'm not sure, I usually see the future."

"Fine. Keep her here, protect her."

"What will you do?" Portan asked?

"I'm going after Evie."

"You can't go alone, it's suicide."

"I'm not going alone. They'll expect her brother to launch a full scale assault to get her back and that's what he's going to do."

"Jacques…"

"What?"

"Be careful."

"I will."

Chapter Twenty-Four

Yfrey and Verm halted their horses at the edge of the cliff that was overlooking Central City. Yfrey dismounted and stared in amazement at the massive rectangular building that was protruding up from the landscape below.

"Have you ever seen anything like it?" Verm was aghast.

"I have, but not in this world." Yfrey tethered her horse to a tree. This was as far as it was able to accompany them. "I bought my boots in a very similar place, but not as tall."

"So, you think there is a massive demand for shoes in Central City and that tower was built to fulfil that need?" Verm asked dryly, as he tethered his horse.

"No, I think Calim has built what he believes is an impenetrable tower fortress. I also think that we'll prove him wrong."

"The bigger they are, the harder they fall," Verm agreed, fingering the hilt of his sword.

"Alright, we'll go on foot down the mountain. Stay close to me and we'll blend into the trees."

"We'd better not go into the city tonight," Verm warned. "Curfew will be in effect and we'll be too conspicuous."

"Alright, we'll wait at the edge of the forest until people come out."

"Do you think the seer is in the tower?"

"It seems the most likely place."

"We'll have to figure out a way to get in then."

"We have to get there first. One step at a time."

"Alright, let's go."

They started to make their way silently down the mountain. It was dark and sharp brambles and roots marred their path. Yfrey could sense her way around the natural obstacles, but Verm was big and awkward and he cursed every time a bramble tore at his skin.

"Stop!" Yfrey hissed urgently as they approached the edge of the wooded area. The light from two torches shone beyond the trees. They were moving towards them at quite a pace, but were still some distance away yet.

"Do you want to hide?" Verm asked in a tone which implied he was not in favour of this course of action.

"There are only two of them, let's wait and see which way they go." Yfrey spoke quietly, never taking her eyes off the moving lights.

Then, what seemed like a thunderously loud snapping of twigs and branches came hurtling towards them. Yfrey moved as close as possible to the trees and made herself invisible. Verm drew his sword and stood strong, waiting. A small boy of around ten or eleven came hurtling towards them, tripped on a root and landed heavily at Verm's feet. Verm scooped up the small child by the lapel and pulled him up close to his hideously scarred face.

"If you want to survive this night be very quiet and stand behind me," he spoke in an audible whisper. Putting the child down, he placed both hands on the hilt of his massive sword and braced himself for battle. The child scurried behind Verm's enormous legs and peered out nervously.

"He went this way, I saw him!" One of the soldiers screamed and the other scrambled noisily through the brush towards the place where Verm awaited them, weapon drawn. They stopped upon witnessing the towering figure of Verm in their path. The men looked at each other, confused. Should they retreat, or challenge this mountain of a man? Verm did not give them much time to ponder.

"So, the army is chasing down children now?" he demanded. "Surely there is a better use of our resources than this."

"Who the hell are you?" One soldier responded aggressively.

Verm grabbed the man's torch bearing arm and pulled the light close so that it illuminated his face. Under the light of the flame, Verm's scar and disfigured features made him appear truly terrifying.

"Who do you think I am?"

"G-g-g-general Verm?" Verm's terrifying features and awesome skill and ruthlessness in battle was the stuff of legend throughout all the battalions.

"That's right, Private. Now, which one of you idiots is going to answer my question?"

"He's out after curfew."

"I can see that. I think my next question has to be, who cares?"

"High Chancellor Calim, Sir." The man sounded distinctly nervous. "He passed a decree that anyone out after curfew should be caught and punished, no exceptions."

"Well, I don't see the high chancellor out here in the middle of the night chasing after children."

"Well, no, you wouldn't, Sir. Since he had the tower built he never leaves it."

"Then how would he know if you just let this boy go? He's not a threat to anything is he?"

"He knows everything! He has a seer Sir."

"What if I told you that the seer can't see anything that's happening here at this moment?"

"What do you mean?" the other soldier asked incredulously.

"It's true," Yfrey said, stepping out of the shadows and lowering her hood so that the men could see her white hair shimmering in the moonlight. She wanted them to know exactly who and what she was. "I have blocked the seer's view of us. And before you get any ideas let me assure you that Verm and I make quite formidable advisories."

"You're working with a witch?"

"Yes."

"To what end?"

"To restore a balance to our world."

"How can we help?"

Verm sighed and sheathed his sword. "Do you think that there are many men who would be willing to join our cause?"

"I think most would be willing to follow you, General."

"Good, spread the word discretely. Those who want to stand alongside me need to be ready. Do nothing until you hear from me."

"What about the boy?"

"You lost him in the woods. Only a boy, not worth the trouble of further pursuit. We will return him to his family. Are we likely to encounter more guards?"

"No, Sir. He escaped our region, there is no-one else patrolling it."
"Alright. Wait to hear from me."
"Yes, Sir."

* * *

"How do we know we can trust them?" Yfrey asked quietly as they moved through the shadows, allowing the boy to lead them to where they hoped he lived.
"We don't know that we can trust anyone." Verm said, his eyes darting vigilantly around the empty streets. "But we have to form alliances; we can't win this thing on our own."
"You're right."
The boy, who had not spoken a word the whole time, stopped outside a house. It looked grubby and reeked of poverty. This is what had become of the ordinary people living in Central City. Verm banged on the weak wooden door so hard that Yfrey was afraid it would come off the hinges. A terrified looking woman opened the door. She looked up at Verm in fear and awe.
"Did you lose something?" Verm asked indicating the still silent child.
"Fortum!" the woman exclaimed, pulling the boy close to her. "I am so sorry, Sir. I don't know how he got out. Please don't punish him, he meant no harm I'm sure."
"We aren't going to punish him, we're just returning him to you," Verm assured her.
"Oh, well! Won't you come in, please? I have baked biscuits, you are welcome to them."
Yfrey and Verm were both extremely hungry, having had their last meal so rudely interrupted, they required little persuasion.
Yfrey helped Fortum's mother in the kitchen whilst Verm sat in the living room with the boy. He took a piece of firewood from the hearth and quickly and expertly carved it into a horse using his knife.
"That's really good, did you carve that?" Fortum's mother asked as she and Yfrey re-entered the room carrying trays.

“I did,” Verm said, offering it to Fortum, who took it without a word and started playing with it in a corner.

“It’s good, you have a lot of talent,” Yfrey said.

“Well, there’s not much call for it in the army,” Verm said awkwardly. He was unused to compliments. “Not very talkative is he?” he added.

“He hasn’t said a word since his sister was taken,” his mother said sadly.

“Taken?” Yfrey asked. She knew what the woman meant but wanted more information.

“Everyone accused of witchcraft has been rounded up and imprisoned in Central Tower. My husband has managed to get himself a job on the cleaning crew, hoping he can find out where she’s being held, but nothing yet.”

“Is she magical?” Yfrey asked, already formulating a plan in her mind.

“Only low level. Sometimes it’s as though she knows what you’re feeling, but nothing that could be seen as a threat to anyone.”

“I might be able to cast a spell to trace her location if I can centre in on her powers.”

“You won’t be able to, I tried. The prison level has some sort of force field around it. It’s as though it doesn’t exist.”

“It must be the seer.” Yfrey said thoughtfully. “Can your husband get us inside with his cleaning crew?”

“I could,” said a man, entering the room from upstairs and looking at his wife’s guests suspiciously. “But why would you want to go in there?”

“So that we can kill the seer and start a revolution.” Yfrey said flatly.

“What is wrong with you?” Verm looked at her in disbelief. “That is not what we tell people!”

“But it’s the truth.”

Verm just looked at her blankly. He had no answer to that.

“I’ll get you in, but then you’re on your own.” The man said calmly. “I’ll get you some overalls, we’ll need to leave soon.”

Chapter Twenty-Five

"But you know that if they have Yfrey there is a good chance that she won't be able to maintain the cloak that's concealing us. They'll see us coming a ricon off," Torius objected.

"I'm counting on it." Jacques said firmly. "What's the matter, Tom? I thought you liked attention?"

"You're asking me to take these men on a suicide mission. Not even I'm that crazy."

"So, you're telling me that you haven't trained them well enough to face a few soldiers. If I'd known you were all mouth I'd have trained them myself."

"They can do it. We can do it. I just want to know what you think it will achieve."

"Didn't you hear what I said? They have Evie! This is how we're going to get her back and I need you to stop fighting me on it, please."

"Don't you see? The second they see me leading an army into Central City they'll kill her. That's if we get as far as Central City. If they see us coming they'll send troops to intercept us."

"Not if they don't see you until you're right on their doorstep."

"And how do you intend to pull off that little miracle?"

"With her." Jacques indicated Borana, who had been standing in the corner, quietly listening to the conversation.

"She can't cloak a whole army. Only Yfrey is powerful enough to do that."

"I have no intention of cloaking anything," Borana said calmly.

"What are you going to do then? Hide us under a massive blanket you knitted yourself?"

"Will you stop being such a complete arse, please? If the next thing that comes out of your mouth isn't helpful, then I swear I will cut off your testicles and wear them as a trophy around my neck! Clear?"

Torius swallowed hard. He had been challenging Jacques' authority a lot recently and she had been tolerating him because there was nothing immediately at stake. Now there was and he had found her limit.

"Please sit down and explain it to him." She spoke in a more measured tone to Borana.

"Did you think that the portal you used to cross worlds just appeared? That it was a naturally occurring phenomenon?"

"I never really gave it any thought." Torius admitted.

"Big surprise there," Jacques muttered.

"They are created by spellbinders who have a specific destination in mind. They go one way only and you would need to open a new portal from the other side to get back, but you won't need to."

"What do you mean?"

"I have been studying the structure and density of the portals for years. I believe I will be able to create one. I've done it once before."

"So we will literally rain hell right in the middle of Central City?" Torius was starting to like this plan.

"You attack the fortress," Jacques said, taking back control of the meeting. "She will open a separate portal for me, wherever Evie is. Once I have her safe we will let you in and take the tower. Calim has forced our hand by taking Evie, but this will work. They will be so focused on attacking you that they won't expect an attack from the inside. They won't know what's hit them."

"I'll go and prepare the men." Torius stood up decisively. "How soon can you have the portal ready?"

"I'll get started on it right now."

"Jacques," he said as he was leaving, "I do love my sister, I just see the bigger picture."

"There is no bigger picture. Get the men ready."

"Jacques," Borana said quietly.

"What is it?" Jacques looked up from preparing her knife for battle.

"Sometimes I see the past too…"
"What use is that?"
"Sometimes it just helps to understand someone."
"Well, maybe when all this works out you can become a therapist."
"I just wanted to say that I'm sorry for what happened to you."
Jacques hesitated. "That was a lifetime ago, I'm a different person now."
"If you need to talk…"
"I'm fine, get to work on the portal."

* * *

Portan seated himself opposite Jacques in front of the fire. He began to set up the Boxcha board for a game.

"I really don't have time for a game at the moment."

"No, I can see that you have a lot of brooding to do. I just thought I'd set it up for later."

"I'm not brooding, I'm thinking."

"You don't have to be strong all the time you know."

"Yes, I do. I didn't want this you know. I don't even know how it happened. My life just spiralled from one hell into another. With this one I have no clue what I'm supposed to be doing and all those people look to me for leadership. I'm not a leader; I'm making this up as I go along. It's like no-one's noticed."

"You know what you're doing. You're decisive, dynamic and you have a strong sense of right and wrong. Yfrey would not have risked her life for you if she did not believe that you can do this. She put her faith in you, and I for one trust her implicitly."

"I trust Evie, of course I do. I can't do this without her. Can't you see that I'm terrified? What if I mess this up and lose her? How will I know what to do next? I can't go back to what I was, I know too much now. I'm babbling."

"You're frightened. I understand. I also believe that you are the most capable woman I have ever met. You can do this."

"You think?"

"I know. And I need you to do something for me."

"What's that?"

"Bring my son home. I can't lose him again."

"Vern is strong and self-assured. He'll be fine," she paused. "But I'll do my best to make sure he gets home to you."

"Then I know he will. Now, I think you have time for a game of Boxcha before you leave."

Jacques smiled. "Sure, why not?" She rearranged her foot soldiers and separated the king. "Your move."

Chapter Twenty-Six

Yfrey and Verm were wearing the cleaning overalls and following single file into the massive black building. Yfrey covered her distinctive hair with a scarf and both of them kept their heads down. Once they passed the guarded checkpoint, their accomplice turned to them and said in a whisper;

"Alright, word is that the seer is on the top floor. How you get out again is on you."

"Thank you for your help."

"I didn't help you, I've never met you."

"Understood."

Due to the fitted nature of their outfits, they had only been able to bring one dagger each. This was no problem for Yfrey, who only ever carried her dagger and the book, but Verm felt almost naked. As soon as they were out of view of people he drew his blade and clung to it.

"Can you sense where he is?" he hissed, scanning the corridor for guards.

"Not yet." Yfrey cocked her head trying to sense the dark powers that the seer was harnessing.

"I don't suppose it would be the door at the end with the eye on it?" Verm asked incredulously.

"Who would be that stupid?"

"Perhaps Calim didn't take the leadership test before taking power? You don't need intelligence to be hateful and charismatic."

"Alright then, let's see what's behind the door with the eye."

Verm tested the handle. The door opened to Corsah's potion room.

"You shouldn't have come," he said nervously from behind his work bench.

"Well, it certainly wasn't in your best interests," Verm said snidely. "Now, you can come with us right now, or I can kill you. Simple as that."

"They knew you were coming, guards will be on the way now. You can't escape, no-one can escape."

"We can if you help us," Yfrey said, watching the corridor nervously.

Corsah looked around the room nervously, then made a snap decision. "Alright, let's go."

They hurried along the corridor. There was a window at the end which had a balcony.

"There's a ladder at the bottom of that window," Corsah indicated. "They are on every level in case of fires."

"Good, get him out of here, fast." Yfrey said firmly to Verm.

"Where are you going?" Verm demanded.

"Calim's holding magical prisoners here and I intend to liberate them."

"It's too dangerous." Verm held Corsah firmly by the back of the neck as he spoke. "We should all stay together."

"Excellent idea," Fosk said stepping through one of the doors. "I think I have a cell big enough for the three of you. Verm, I expected better of you. Why are you associating with witches?"

"I have never concerned myself with what you expect of me, Fosk. Sufficient to say that I do not like being lied to, and I like the brand on my father's chest even less. If I find out you had anything to do with that I will inflict a special type of pain on you."

"You are in no position to be making threats, Verm. You are my prisoner."

"That was a promise. And I doubt very much that you could best me in battle, and there are three of us."

"I don't want to fight you Verm," Fosk smiled in false friendliness. "I'll leave that to the GUARDS!"

Ten or fifteen men came charging from the same door Fosk had used, weapons drawn.

"Get down that ladder and go straight to B-Battalion," Verm hissed to Corsah. "Tell them that the General said it's time, we'll cover you. GO!"

Corsah scurried to the window. Yfrey and Verm protected his escape. Yfrey wasn't skilled in combat and ducked and dodged, scratching with her knife where the opportunity arose. Verm had quickly disarmed one guard and was fighting with both a sword and a dagger. It became very clear to Fosk that fifteen to two was not as good odds as he had originally thought. He quickly ascertained, however, that Yfrey was the weak link in Verm's army of two. Deftly he moved through the fight and grabbed her from behind, holding her own knife to her throat.

"Verm!" he called loudly. "I have your witch!"

They all stopped to look at him. "Put your weapons down and I won't kill her."

Verm held out his weapons at arm's length from his body and slowly lowered them to the ground.

"What are you doing?" Yfrey demanded. "I'm not important."

"You are important to me," Verm said, dropping slowly to his knees and placing the weapons on the ground next to him. He put his hands behind his head, the whole time looking at Yfrey. Fosk nodded and one of the guards struck him on the back of the skull with the hilt of his sword.

"No!" Yfrey cried, starting to struggle violently.

"Quiet witch!" Fosk cried, pulling the knife harder against her throat. "Bring him," he commanded the guards, "there's room in the cell for two." He dragged Yfrey along a corridor and down some stairs to a dark, oppressive room at the end. Releasing her, he kicked her hard in the base of the spine, sending her sprawling onto the hard stone floor face first. The guards dropped Verm behind her and she heard the loud click of the locking mechanism as the door was locked behind them.

Yfrey rolled onto her back and pushed herself up into a seated position. The room was dark; the windows were boarded; whoever had prepared the room clearly did not want outside magic getting in. There was a small single bed against the wall with an itchy looking woollen blanket, and a pillow in a case. Glancing across at Verm, in the half-light that forced itself through the gaps in the boards and under the crack of the door, Yfrey could see that he was bleeding from where he had been struck on the cranium. She struggled to her feet and hurried over to the bed. Removing the pillowcase, she ripped it lengthways and folded it over on itself to form a bandage. Lifting his head, she bound his wound tightly to stop the bleeding.

“Wake up!” she slapped his face hard. “Wake up! You’re too big and heavy for me to lift onto the bed so you’ll have to get yourself up there! Wake up!”

Verm opened his eyes groggily. “My angel of mercy!” he said sardonically.

“I’ve never claimed to be an angel. Can you get yourself onto the bed?”

“I think so,” he said, struggling to his feet. “Are you alright?”

“Fine. You know that was a very stupid thing to do?”

“Don’t you think it was romantic?”

“No, definitely not.”

“Well, I’ve never been a romantic figure. What do you think our next move should be?”

“You get some rest. They can’t leave us in here indefinitely. When they open that door we need to be ready. If we can get to that window I can use my magic and we can get out of here.”

“Right. Get you through the door and to the window. I can do that.”

“I know you can. You’re very capable, if a hopeless romantic!” Yfrey smiled at him. “Get some rest.”

“Yes ma’am.”

Chapter Twenty-Seven

"So, this is gonna bring me out exactly where Evie is?" Jacques looked suspiciously at the portal.

"I focused on her magic, so unless someone else has that signature, you will come out within arm's length of her." Borana assured her.

"But there's no way to know how many guards are with her? I mean, I could be jumping into a hornet's nest, right?"

"Well, if Torius has done his job properly then they will be entirely too busy to waste time guarding her."

"You think I've given him long enough?" Jacques asked Portan, who was circling the portal with fascination.

"I think it's now or never," he said earnestly.

"Right," Jacques said, bracing herself and gripping her knife.

"Remember," Borana spoke urgently to Jacques. "You'll need to hold your breath before you enter the portal because there is no air inside. You'll only be in there about ten-seconds, but if you try to breathe and can't you are likely to come out in a panic and be more vulnerable."

"Gotcha. Hold breath." Jacques took on the portal as if she were embarking on a judo roll; blocking her face with her left arm and holding her right out in front of her ready to hit the ground. Her knife was in her belt. Holding her breath, she leapt into the portal. For what seemed like much longer than ten-seconds, she was surrounded by different coloured lights and an amazing feeling of floating. Then, very suddenly she wasn't. She hit the hard stone floor with her right hand first before rolling onto her back and hitting her left hand next to her to absorb some to the shock. The heavy landing forced her to expel the breath she had been holding before leaping to her feet and drawing her dagger and looking around. Yfrey turned from where she had been attempting to unboard the windows.

"Jacques!"

"Hey! I thought I told you to be careful! You call getting yourself locked in this grimy place being careful?"

"Well, it was Verm's fault, he suddenly decided to try and be noble." Yfrey teased, indicating the giant man who was now sitting on the bed with his feet on the floor, observing the reunion quietly.

"Did you want me to let them kill you?" he asked in mock irritation. "Because I can call them back now and say it's OK after all."

"Vern, you look like a land girl, what's that thing on your head?"

"It's a bandage!" Yfrey said defensively. "He cut his head when he was being noble."

"I thought I'd try and look more like you," Verm snorted. "And I see you wanted to look more like me," he indicated the scar on Jacques' cheek.

"You hurt yourself?" Yfrey reached out and gently touched the scar to see how deep it went.

"No," Jacques pushed her hand away. "Some soldiers provoked by your idiot brother hurt me. But it doesn't hurt anymore."

"All the best people have scars," Verm said reassuringly.

"You know, I heard that somewhere. So, what are we doing, unblocking this window?"

"Yes, there's a lot of noise outside and I wanted to see what was going on."

"If everything's going as planned, then a revolution's going on," Jacques said as she wedged her knife under the boards and used it as a lever to pry them away from the window.

Below them was what appeared to be chaos. The small band of rebels Torius had led through the portal had been joined by people from the streets. Market vendors, street sweepers, all sorts had taken up arms and were trying to break into the tower. The guards who were based inside the Central Tower were now outside, battling to protect the entrance.

"I don't know how long Torius will be able to hold out against trained soldiers," Yfrey confessed. "He thinks he's much better than he is."

“He won’t have to hold out long,” Verm said confidently. “See that mass moving over that hill? Those are my men; he just has to hold out until they get here.”

“And we’re on the inside, so we can take this tower,” Jacques said confidently. “That will be a crippling blow to Calim’s empire, he’ll need to regroup and give us time to secure our base of operations. If only we could get out of this damn room,” she added less confidently.

“If we could get this window open then I think I could get us out,” Yfrey said, pulling at the handle, which must have been welded shut.

“Here!” Verm threw the pillow at her from across the room. “Hold a side each against that window.”

Both Jacques and Yfrey held a side of the pillow, standing opposite sides of the window frame. Jacques raised her eyebrows quizzically at Yfrey, who shrugged.

Verm took a step back, then, using his vast body mass he punched the pillow. The glass was reinforced and did not shatter. Instead the frame came away from the bricks that were holding it and the whole thing plummeted to the earth below.

“Oh, shit!” Jacques exclaimed, peering out to see if anyone was hurt. Two soldiers were lying under the now shattered debris of the window. Torius was standing over them, looking up to see where the missile had come from. Upon seeing Jacques he grinned and saluted before joining back in with the battle.

“I swear that guy was born under a lucky star!” she exclaimed in disbelief.

“Right, you ready to get out of here?” Yfrey asked.

“Do it lady!”

“Stand with your backs against the wall.”

Duly Jacques and Verm pressed themselves against the wall and waited to see what Yfrey was going to do. Calling upon the elements, Yfrey drew a powerful wind through the gap in the wall. It sent the door flying off its hinges and smashing into the opposite wall of the corridor, which appeared deserted.

"What now?" Yfrey looked to Jacques for guidance.

"Well, um…" Jacques looked at her knife awkwardly, wishing that some evil minion would attack and distract her from her current dilemma. "You know," she said defensively. "I dive through a portal at great risk to my personal well-being to rescue you two, it might be nice to have some gratitude."

"You don't have a plan, huh?"

"I suggest that we find Calim and force a surrender." Verm offered.

"Good plan! Where would you suggest we look?"

"Am I interrupting something important?" Fosk asked, stepping out of one of the doors.

"Not really," Jacques said pleasantly. "Say, could you tell me where Calim is? He's, well, what would you say Vern?"

"Oh, about five-ten, ginger hair, whiny little voice that makes you just wanna punch him in the face."

"That's a nice headband Verm, anything that hides a portion of your face is an improvement."

"That's kind of you to say; perhaps I could buy you a drink when this is all over."

"Stop!" Yfrey said urgently.

"What's the matter? Jealous? I only want him for his body, I promise." Verm was being sarcastic but he never took his eyes off Fosk. He was prepared for any sudden move.

"He's trying to distract us, don't you see?"

"Is that true, Fosk?" Verm demanded, suddenly grabbing him by the throat and lifting him as though he weighed nothing.

"I don't know what you're talking about!" Fosk wheezed.

"Sure you do." Verm said squeezing his throat tighter.

Fosk reached into his belt and pulled Yfrey's knife out. He was about to stab Verm, when he felt Jacques' blade pressing just below his ribs.

"I really wouldn't do that," she said firmly, taking the knife from him. "Isn't this yours?"

"Thanks, I was wondering where I left that. Last time I saw it, it was at my throat."

"Put him down," Jacques said determinedly. Verm instantly released his grip, dropping Fosk two feet to the ground.

"You know who I am?" Jacques demanded, pressing the tip of the knife so firmly against Fosk's throat that she drew blood. Fosk nodded. "Then you know what I'm capable of. So do me a favour and tell me where Calim is."

"You're too late Roghnaithe, it's done. It less than twenty minutes we will all be dead."

"What's he talking about?" Jacques looked to Verm.

"The fail safe, Calim must have set the building to blow up rather than have it taken by us."

"I don't know who's crazier!" Jacques exclaimed, "Him, or you for volunteering to stay behind and die just to keep us here."

"Death is nothing compared to what Calim does to those who fail him," Fosk coughed.

"Well, you'll just have to stick with us then," Jacques said firmly. "We're getting out of here, now!"

"Wait!" Yfrey cried urgently. "What about the prisoners?"

"What prisoners?"

"Calim's been taking magical prisoners and keeping them here somewhere; we have to get them out."

"Fine," Jacques said before turning back to Fosk. "Where are they?"

"He keeps them in the basement. That's all I can tell you. No-one's allowed down there, not even me."

"Right, Vern, get him out of here, we'll go break them out."

"No, I'll go alone." Yfrey said.

"No, we should stick together," Verm spoke at the same time.

"No and no." Jacques said steadily. "I need you to get out and clear the blast radius. And if we don't get out I need you to lead the revolution, we can't have that arrogant git in charge, there's no telling what would happen. Besides, I promised your father I'd get you out in one piece." Verm nodded, took Fosk by the back of the neck and briskly marched him out. "And as for you," Jacques continued turning to Yfrey. "I left you alone and look what happened. You made a revolution and blew up a building!"

"Well, technically that was you."

"We don't have time, we have to find this basement and get out before this whole place blows." She grabbed Yfrey's hand and started to run towards the staircase, "I presume the basement is at the bottom of a building in your world too?"

"Usually," Yfrey panted, trying to keep up. "And if I had to guess I'd say it's through that door." She pointed. It was vast with several locks and strange symbols painted on it in red.

"What do they mean?" Jacques asked.

"Superstition, supposed to block magic, but if the prisoners believed them it might stop them from attempting to escape."

"Right, well, let's get it open." Jacques drew her blade. She was going to try and pick the lock with it, but as she removed it from its sheath it glowed a bright gold and some sort of energy passed through it and blasted through the door.

"How did you do that?"

"Not a clue!" Jacques stared briefly at the blade before returning it to the sheath in her belt. "No time to wonder, let's move." They hurried down the stairs to the bottom of the basement. It was very dark.

"Hello? Is there anyone down here?" Jacques called.

"Éadrom!" Yfrey said loudly, clapping her hands twice. The whole place glowed with a gentle yellow light.

"That's a neat trick."

"Something my parents taught me. There's no-one here," Yfrey sounded frightened. "We should just go."

"Wait, what's that?" Jacques indicated something flickering in the corner. "It can't be, can it?"

Tentatively they moved closer. It was a portal.

"He's been sending the prisoners through a portal."

"So what do we do?"

"I say we get out of here. Wherever they are, they're safe from the blast radius, and we aren't. We can come back for them when it's safe and we have more people. After all, we don't know where that comes out."

"Agreed." Yfrey nodded. "Let's go."

They moved quickly towards the stairs when there was a deafening BOOM that Jacques had heard once before, the day she lost her brother.

"Oh shit!"

A wall of flames herded them in the other direction. Without even thinking, they leapt through the portal and out of reach of the fire wall.

* * *

Gasping for breath, Jacques found herself lying in lush grass. The sun was warm on her face and birds were singing in the trees. In the far distance overhead was a big blue mountain and she could hear a stream trickling somewhere close by.

"Evie?" she called as she struggled to her feet. "Evie, are you here?"

"Over here!" Yfrey called. She had landed in a bush and was struggling to stand. A small collection of woodland animals, who, clearly, until this point, had resided in the bush were chattering irritably at her.

"Oh dear!" Jacques laughed, taking her hand and hauling her up. "Well, at least you had a soft landing." She reached over and removed a twig from Yfrey's hair.

"Yes," Yfrey said, brushing herself off. "Although I'm not sure these little creatures appreciated having their home squashed."

"Well, hopefully they're insured. Do you know where we are?"

"Absolutely no idea. It seems nice though."

"Yeah, right. I mean anywhere has got to be better than being blown up, right?"

"It doesn't seem like the sort of place Calim would send prisoners though does it? I mean, it's quite pleasant."

"I dunno, I mean, the guy is nuts, right? Maybe this is his idea as hell. Or maybe he just didn't care where they went as long as it was away from him. Who knows?"

"Maybe, I'm not sure." Yfrey spoke thoughtfully.

"Well, come on. Let's go and have a look around, see where we are."

"Alright, but we should be careful. We don't know anything about this place."

"Yeah, course. Come on." Jacques seemed oddly enthusiastic about this new place and Yfrey was suspicious.

"Are you alright?"

"Fine, why?"

"I don't know, you're usually more cautious than this."

"Evie, I'm happy to be alive. I can't remember the last time I was. I'm happy to be alive and I'm happy you're here to share it with me." She gave Yfrey a hug.

Taken aback Yfrey lightly reciprocated the hug looking out over Jacques' shoulder.

"Jacques…" She began uncertainly.

"Yeah?" Jacques released her grip and looked at her.

"What's that?" Yfrey pointed at the sky, something was coming towards them. Something big.

"Holy shit!" Jacques exclaimed in utter amazement. "I think that's a dragon!"

Part Three: Circles in Time

Chapter Twenty-Eight

"Torius! Stop teasing your sister and come in for dinner!" Guera called from the doorway.

"Mum! I'm not teasing her, we're playing!"

"I think she'd see it differently. Now, untie her and bring her in or I'll tell your father!"

"Tell me what?" Kowour walked up the path to the cottage and kissed his wife.

"He's tied Yfrey to that tree again, I don't know why he can't just play nicely."

"I'll speak to him, we didn't raise him to be a bully; I don't know why he does it."

"Calim's mother said he's been using his magic to tease him again; I don't know what happened, but he and his friends are so unkind to that boy, I do feel sorry for him."

"I'll have a word, I promise, he's a good boy, just needs guidance."

"Tell her!" Torius pushed Yfrey forward in front of their mother.

"It was just a game."

"Alright, Sweetheart, come in and help me with dinner."

"Not you, Son," Kowour caught his son's shoulder. "Come over here with me, we need to talk."

He led Torius to a fallen tree that served as a garden bench and sat down.

Aw, Dad, we were just playing, she doesn't mind, honest."

"Why is it that your games never involve you being tied to a tree?"

"If I'm tied to a tree then who would rescue Yfrey?"

"She wouldn't need rescuing if you hadn't tied her to a tree. And, what's this your mother tells me about you bullying Calim? You know he has no powers, you shouldn't pick on the weak, you should defend them."

"He's creepy, Dad. I came up on him cutting up a dead fox. I bet he killed it too."

"Well, that may be," Kowour disguised his disgust at this piece of information as best he could. "In which case you should stay away from him. I need you to stop stirring up trouble, we're trying to live peacefully here."

"I bet that's what the fox said until that creep stabbed it to death and started exploring its innards."

"Please, Son. Can't you just try to stay away from him?"

"Sure, Dad."

"And give your sister a break, she really loves you, you know?"

"I know; I'm only playing with her."

"Well, play nicer."

* * *

"You don't have to defend him, I know you don't like playing that tree game," Guera said, as she and Yfrey set the table.

"I know, but no-one really likes him, and I want him to know that I'm on his side."

"People would like him more if he wasn't such a bully. I don't know where we went wrong with him."

"Mum, you didn't do anything, it's just who he is. We can't change him."

"I hope you're wrong, otherwise he will turn into a very dangerous young man."

"He's not dangerous to us, he loves us."

"I know. Did you study the book today?"

"Yes. I still don't understand that prophecy; a great darkness will envelope the world, what does that mean?"

"The strange thing about prophecies is that they seldom make sense until after the event. Foresight is often a curse rather than a blessing. Here, I want you to have something." She unlocked a wooden casket that Yfrey had not seen before and withdrew a sheathed knife with a slightly curved blade.

"A knife?"

“This knife has been passed down through the women in our family for generations. It is attuned to our magic and will protect and guide you in the future.”

“I have you for that.”

“Well, I won’t always be here.”

“Hey, what’s that?” Torius barged into the kitchen. “You giving her a knife? I want a knife. I’m the oldest, I should get a knife.”

“That knife was not meant for you. Now sit down and eat your dinner.”

“She’ll give it to me anyway.”

“No, I won’t.” Yfrey spoke with a calm firmness that she had never used with her brother before. He was taken aback.

“OK, sorry. I was just joking.”

“Well, not everything is a joke.”

“I know, sorry.”

Guera and Kowour smiled at each other. The path was set.

After dinner Yfrey headed to the small copse just beyond the far ridge, where she knew Calim would be. Sure enough the boy was there, alone, hitting some bushes with a stick.

“Hey Calim, you OK?”

“Go away, Witch!”

“Look, I’m sorry about my brother. He can be really horrible sometimes, but he doesn’t mean it. He just doesn’t think.”

“I said go away! I hate you! I hate all of you! I hate all of you! Leave me alone!”

“Alright, I’m sorry. I didn’t want to upset you, I just wanted to make sure you were alright.”

“You didn’t upset me. None of you can upset me!”

“Alright, well, I’m glad you aren’t upset.”

“No, but your brother will be!” And with that he hit Yfrey hard on the head with the stick, cutting her eye.

“Ow!” she cried out. “What are you doing? Leave me alone!” She stepped backwards as he prodded her in the stomach with the stick. “Ow! Stop it!”

He raised the stick above his head to hit her again, but a strong male hand caught it and wrenched it from his grasp.

"Go home." Wrance said firmly, looking down at the angry little child, whose cheeks were as red as his fiery hair. He ran away in tears. "You should stay away from that boy, Yfrey." Wrance said, as he dropped the stick and scooped her up in his arms. "There's something not quite right about him."

"Torius was mean to him, I just wanted to make sure he was alright."

"I don't know what to say, Yfrey. Sometimes being kind isn't rewarded. It should be, but it isn't." He knocked on the door of the cottage and Guera answered.

"Yfrey! What happened?"

"It was that sad little magicless boy. He had a stick. I arrived before too much harm was done," Wrance said, reassuringly.

"Thank you, Wrance. Will you come in for a drink?"

"Yfrey!" Kowour exclaimed upon seeing his daughter. "What happened?"

"It's alright, Dad. Calim was just upset, I'll stay away from him in the future."

"He's not as upset as he will be!" Torius said angrily, getting to his feet and storming out the cottage.

"Torius! Get back here now!" Guera cried angrily, but he was already gone.

"I'll get him," Wrance said firmly. "We need to have a talk anyway."

"Come on Yfrey, let's get you cleaned up," Kowour said, scooping his daughter up and carrying her to the kitchen.

"Dad, I don't want Torius to hurt Calim. He's bigger than him, and Calim is just sad. If he gets hurt he'll just be angry, it won't fix anything."

"I know. Your brother is very strong, but don't worry, Wrance will catch him."

"He'll catch him this time, but we can't keep him in a cave. Dad, I'm frightened of him."

"Don't be frightened of him, he'll never hurt you."

"Not on purpose."

"Come on, let's get you to bed."

* * *

"Torius!" Wrance called as he caught up with him.

"What do you want Old Man?"

"I'm not that old, but I've got a damn sight more life experience than you."

"So, what? You gonna tell me that I shouldn't teach that little twerp a lesson? Make him think he can hurt my sister and get away with it?"

"This isn't about your sister. This is about you and how angry you are. What happened to make you so angry?"

"Didn't you see what he did to Yfrey? I don't understand why you aren't angry."

"You were angry before that happened to your sister. I wonder if you even remember what it's like to feel anything else."

"So, what? You gonna take me home now?"

"Revenge is a cycle, Torius. It will never stop unless someone stops it. You need to stop it."

"That's what I'm going to do. He won't touch her again when I'm done."

"You think you're so big and strong? Well, there is always someone bigger and stronger, and if you don't learn that soon, then you will die a violent death, very young."

"You don't know what you're talking about."

Wrance was well muscled and fit from working on the land. He punched Torius in the stomach, just hard enough to knock the wind out of him. Torius looked at him in disbelief. He did not know what to do.

"What? You not going to fight back?"

"You're a grown up…"

"So?"

"I get it."

"Good. Let's channel your energies into something useful. I'll pick you up at dawn tomorrow and you can come and work in the fields with me. It'll do you good to learn a trade and some discipline. Come on, let's get you home."

Torius was defeated and followed Wrance home in silence.

Chapter Twenty-Nine

"So, we going clubbing tonight?" Karen asked as she bit into her sandwich.

"I can't tonight. My stupid brother is back from college so we have to have a family dinner." Jacques took a swig of her cola and looked down rather disappointedly at her school dinner. "Do we know what this is?"

"I think it's lasagne… don't quote me though." Karen prodded the substance on her plate uncertainly. "Dude, you should pack a sandwich, seriously."

"Yeah, really. Oh my gosh! Don't look now but Tommy is totally checking you out!"

"Really?" Karen glanced in the reflection of her knife. "How's my makeup?"

"Good. You wearing that cherry bomb sparkle I leant you?"

"I so am. Don't you think I look kissable?"

"Quick! He's coming over! Pretend we're… so, yeah, my brother, oh, hi Tommy."

"Jacques, Karen, you girls gonna be at The Rave tonight? It's eighteen to twenty-three night. Should be cool."

"I can't, my brother's home and we're doing a family thing. But Karen was just saying that she'd like to go out tonight."

"Yeah, Jacques let me down, you may be my hero!"

"Well, club doesn't open 'til ten, if you can get out early you should totally come."

"I'll see if I can cut out early. I'll text you."

"Awesome, see you later."

"He is too cute! Are you interested?" Karen asked as she watched Tommy walk away.

"No, he's not really my type."

"Well, you won't mind if I make my move!"

"Feel free. Hey, you want me to not be able to come tonight?"

"Oh no! The evening isn't complete without you. Besides, I'm not that easy! It'll take a few clubbing sessions before I want to be alone with him."

"Cool, OK. Well, I'll text you tonight then, OK?"

"Sure."

* * *

"Hey, Squirt! You didn't have to dress up for me!" Ben teased as Jacques hurried downstairs wearing a mini dress, with sparkly blue heels and matching handbag. Her blonde hair was tied back off her face and she was wearing her cherry bomb lipstick and blue eyeshadow.

"I'm not dressed up for you, Loser! I'm going clubbing with Karen after dinner."

"Not dressed like that you aren't!" Her father said as he walked through the hall.

"Oh, come on, Dad, I'm seventeen. Everyone dresses like this now."

"It's true," Ben said calmly. "She looks very fashionable."

"Thanks Loser! Hey, you should totally come out with us tonight, it'll be fun!"

"Well, I won't look so cute in that dress."

"It wouldn't fit you anyway, you're getting a bit of a belly."

"It's all the fast food. I miss Mum's cooking."

"Well, come and get it then!" their mother called from the dining room.

"This is great, Mum!" Ben said enthusiastically as he tucked into a desert of sticky toffee pudding and custard.

"You know, it's very easy to make," his mother smiled back at him. "You don't need to live on takeaway."

"Hey! What's the rule about phones at the table?" their father demanded as Jacques received a text message.

"It's Karen, she's early," Jacques explained, completely ignoring her father's objection and reading the message.

"That's OK," Ben said between mouthfuls. "Tell her we'll meet her there, I'll drive us."

"Awesome!" Jacques smiled, tapping away at the keys.

“Do you ever wonder why we bother?” their father said to their mother, as he observed the complete lack of respect for the phone at the table rule.

“No, mostly I think what a good job we did raising our children.” She smiled warmly at her husband.

“OK, come on Loser, we need to find you and outfit, you’re never gonna pull in that grandpa jumper!”

“Don’t you think I’m kinda cool and trendy?”

“God! I can’t actually believe you just used the word ‘trendy’!” Jacques rolled her eyes in exasperation at her brother’s total lack of cool. “Come on, let’s see if you’ve got anything remotely decent in your wardrobe.” She took his hand and dragged him upstairs.

Once in the club Jacques scanned around for Karen and Tommy.

“Didn’t you pick a place to meet them?” Ben shouted over the blare of the music.

“You know Karen, she’s not all that reliable, and if she thinks she has a chance with Tommy she won’t be over-keen to find us. She’ll turn up, don’t worry. Let’s dance!”

“Wow, I’m exhausted!” Ben panted across the dance floor. “I don’t know where you get your energy.”

“Well, I don’t live on takeaway for a start, and there’s my kickboxing. Come on, let’s get a drink.”

“Yeah, how’s the kickboxing going?”

“I passed the preliminary rounds, if I get through this weekend then I have a shot at the Under Eighteens’ title.”

“Very cool. Good for you. I’d like to come down and watch if you let me know when it is.”

“Sure thing, I have to get through this weekend first though.”

“You will. Hey, look, there’s a table. You grab it and I’ll get the drinks.”

“OK.”

Jacques seated herself on the stool against the small, round table and searched in her bag for her phone. She wanted to text Karen and let her know they were here. She didn’t look up when a drink was place down in front of her, just reached out and took a swig.

“Hey, I’m just texting Karen to let her know we’re here.”

“Who’s Karen?”

Jacques looked up to see a complete stranger before her, grinning broadly.

"Oh God! I'm sorry! I thought you were my brother! Did I drink your drink? I'll get you a fresh one."

"No, I bought it for you." He smiled at her.

"Oh, that's sweet, thank you. I'm here with my brother, but you're welcome to sit with us. He's tired from dancing."

"Don't tell me you dress like that to go out with your brother! What a waste!"

"Looking nice is never a waste!" Jacques smiled and took another swig of her drink. "What's your name?"

"I'm Stu, how about you?"

"Jacques." She suddenly felt very dizzy and grabbed her head. "Stu, I don't feel so good."

"Wanna go out and get some air?"

"I should wait for Ben…" she swayed uncertainly on her stool.

"Come on, I think you've just had a bit too much to drink, I'll get you outside."

Jacques allowed herself to be lifted off the stool and led outside to the streets.

* * *

"Hey! Look who I ran into!" Ben said cheerily as he headed back to the table, flanked by Karen and Tommy. "Jacques?" He put the drinks down on the table and scanned the teaming club for his sister.

"Maybe she went to dance?" Karen suggested.

"No, she was keeping the table." Ben was concerned.

"Look!" Tommy picked up her handbag from the floor. "She wouldn't have left this here would she?"

"Excuse me," Ben interrupted the table next to them. "Did you see where the girl went who was sitting here?"

"Yeah," the woman smiled at him. "I think she had a bit too much to drink, so her boyfriend took her outside."

"She hadn't had anything to drink!" Ben was worried.

“And she’s never leave with some bloke!” Karen said urgently.

“Come on, let’s see if we can find her,” Tommy led the way pushing through the crowd to the exit.

“Jacques? Jacques?” They called urgently as they hurried around the car-park. Then they heard a cry.

“Jacques! Call the police!” Ben instructed Karen as he hurried towards the sound of the scream closely flanked by Tommy.

Ahead of them they saw a petite woman with bright white, short, spiky hair wrestle a badly beaten man to the ground and pin him under her knee. Upon seeing them approach she called out.

“Help her,” indicating the shadows behind a dustbin, “she needs an ambulance.”

“Jacques!” Ben hurried over to the badly beaten body of his sister, “my God! Jacques!”

“Send an ambulance too! We’ve found her, she’s been attacked!” Karen’s voice was cracking as she spoke to the emergency service operator and hurried after Ben.

“You, boy, come here!” the woman called Tommy as she forced Stu’s face into the concrete. Tommy walked over to her uncertainly. “You came out here, you saw him attack her and you fought him off and detained him until the police arrived. I was never here.”

“What?” Tommy looked at her in disbelief.

“I was never here. He’s unconscious now, he won’t give you any trouble. Come here, take over from me.”

“But Jacques?”

“She’ll live.”

Once Tommy took over straddling the limp body the woman seemed to vanish into the breeze.

* * *

Jacques lay in the hospital bed, staring at the ceiling. She had been interrogated by the police, examined by numerous doctors and photographed from every angle. She felt totally out of control and exposed and did not know where to go from here. Suddenly she was aware of a presence in the doorway of her room.

“It’s you. They said I imagined you, that Tommy saved me, but I know it was you.”

"I'm sorry, I was too late."

"No, you saved me. They said he killed the last girl, that I was lucky." The words stuck in her throat, she didn't feel lucky.

"I just wanted to make sure you were alright, I won't stay."

"No, please come in, talk to me. I'm tired of being on my own."

"Alright." The woman walked uncertainly into the room and seated herself on the chair next to the bed.

"What you did, it was awesome. Was it karate?"

"Something like that. It's a blend of different martial arts and self-defence techniques. Once you have a basic grasp of them you can adapt them to meet your needs. I could teach you."

"Really?"

"Yes. When you're feeling better I'll find you."

Chapter Thirty

Guera hurried to answer the door of the cottage, which sounded as though it were being broken down by rapid pounding.

"Karus! What on Domhain is the matter? You're bleeding!"

"It's not my blood," her sister-in-law hurried into the cottage and shut the door. "It's happened; they've taken the city, we need to act now."

"Slow down, whose blood is that, who has taken the city, what do you want us to do?" Guera seated herself next to her husband at the kitchen table.

"Some soldier. They were there to keep the peace while we were protesting, but then the Right Way attacked us. They have taken Central City, they are moving throughout the country, trying to take local governments. It turned into chaos, the soldiers fought everyone who wasn't in a uniform, the one who came at me isn't so pretty any more. It's time to find the Roghnaithe, we need to prepare ourselves, it's happening now."

"It can't happen now! Yfrey is only fourteen, she isn't ready!"

"I can do it, we don't need to involve Yfrey. Help me create a portal, I'm going through."

* * *

"We should leave now!" Guera's voice was raised in frustration at how obstinate her husband was being.

"If we leave now we'll be giving in to fear. Do you want the children to grow up seeing their parents as people who don't stand up for what they believe in?" Kowour responded with equal zeal.

"I want the children to be able to grow up!"

"Hey!" Yfrey barged into the room. "We aren't children! I'm fourteen and Torius is nineteen and I think that if this argument is about our future then I think we should be involved in it, don't you?"

"I'm sorry, Yfrey." Guera moderated her tone with her daughter. "We aren't arguing, we're discussing, we became a bit too loud. Of course you should both be involved. Go get your brother from the fields and we'll discuss it over dinner."

"Fine." Yfrey did not like being brushed off, but she knew that her mother was not to be argued with.

"Don't forget this," her mother handed her the knife.

As Yfrey headed into the village square, she saw Molek on the podium. Since the Right Way activists had started to become more involved in the political process, Molek had spent most days there, preaching about how magic was unnatural, and how the right way to live was through manmade machinery. Each time she saw him, the crowd around him grew larger and this frightened her. There had already been a number of hate attacks on the magical community, and there had been clashing and rioting in Central City. She pulled her hood up to conceal her hair and walked quickly past. Her main concern was that if he was still there when Torius returned with her, they would get into a fight. Torius was incredibly intolerant of the 'Right Way' movement and was not afraid to show it. His belief in his own infallibility made Yfrey fear for him each time he responded to one of their taunts.

She hurried through the fields of tall grass and maize until she reached the golden cornfield in which Torius and Wrance were working. The sun gleamed down, shining off the corn, and a warm summer breeze brushed her cheek. Here, away from all the hate and negativity, she felt safe. An ear of corn striking her on the side of the face abruptly woke her from her temporary daydream.

"Hey, Sis!" Torius grinned, striding towards her. His shirtless torso glistened with the sweat of the day's manual labour and his face was red from the day's exercise.

"Hey!" she said, picking up the corn and flinging it back at him. "You coming home for dinner? Mum and Dad are arguing again."

"Yeah, sure," he picked up his shirt from the ground and placed a supportive hand on his sister's shoulder. He knew how much the arguments at home upset her.

"Hey, Wrance! I'm heading home for dinner, I'll come back later, OK?"

"Sure!" Wrance called back from the other side of the field. "Hey, Yfrey! Give my best to your folks!"

"Hi Wrance! I will."

Dusk was starting to fall as they headed down the hill and back to their home. Yfrey was leading her brother the long way round deliberately, to avoid the village square. The last thing she needed today was to break up a fight.

"What's that?" she asked, indicating smoke which was billowing up through the trees.

"Looks like something is on fire!" Torius exclaimed, breaking into a run. "Come on! Let's see if we can help!"

Torius was much fitter than his sister from the years of working on the land, and he left her in his wake as he hurtled towards the source of the blaze. Knowing she would never catch him, she turned back to get Wrance, if it was a big fire, they would need all the help they could get.

"Yfrey, what is it?" Wrance asked, looking up from his work.

"There's a fire, you have to help! Torius went on ahead!" Yfrey gasped breathlessly.

"Alright, calm down," Wrance said hastily pulling his shirt on. "Let's go and see if we can help."

By the time they arrived there was barely anything left of the village. Torius stood, staring at what used to be their home. In front of it, implanted in the ground, still burning was a cross; the symbol of the 'Right Way' movement. Yfrey felt both anger and sadness well up inside of her as she surveyed the carnage that lay before them. Almost as though they were echoing her mood, imposing, heavy storm clouds loomed overhead. The rain came down hard and fast, quelling the flames. Yfrey stared in complete despair at what used to be their home.

"What are we going to do now? Where will we go?" she asked. She felt numb, as though she were unable to process what had just happened.

"We should go to the woods," Wrance said quietly, lightly touching her arm. "We'll be safe there for now, until we work out what to do next."

"I don't need to work out anything!" Torius spoke angrily. "I am going to find who did this, and I am going to kill them."

"Not right this second," Wrance said firmly. "We need to regroup, you're no match for anyone at the moment."

"No, but I will be!"
"What are you going to do?"
"You'll see."
"Come on, let's go," Wrance said gently, trying to take Yfrey's arm.
"I need to get the book." Yfrey said, pulling away and moving towards the burnt out house.
"Forget the book!" Torius exclaimed. "What use will it be? We need to get out of here now!"
"It will be of use. It predicted this, it will tell us what to do next. I need it."
"It's probably incinerated with everything else," Torius grumbled, but he was already resigned to his sister going into what was left of the building. "Hurry up then."
Yfrey hurried into the precarious smoke stained shell of a house. Tentatively she mounted the stairs to what used to be her room. In the far corner was the metal lock box in which she kept The Book of Abisan. The box was black from the damage the fire had caused. She took the key from around her neck and unlocked it. The book was wrapped in oil cloth and undamaged by the fire. Quickly, she put it in the inside pocket of her cloak. From outside she could hear shouting. She moved quickly to the window, where she could see Torius kicking Molek, who was lying on the ground. Two men were lying next to him, bleeding from what appeared to be stab wounds. From this distance Yfrey could not tell whether they were still alive. Both Wrance and Torius were holding swords, which they had not previously possessed. Yfrey could only assume that they had belonged to the fallen men.
"Tell me where they are!" Torius spoke vehemently, kicking harder with every word.
"It's too late!" Molek gasped. "They have been taken by the inquisitors to be questioned about their magic."
"Where?" He kicked harder.
"I don't know…"

"Torius," Yfrey spoke quietly coming up behind her brother. "Come on, leave him, he doesn't know anything."

"He did this!" Torius' voice burnt with fury.

"Please, Torius. Let's just go."

"You're lucky," Torius spoke down at the crumpled man. "I ever see you again, I'll kill you."

They hurried away into the forest.

Under the shelter of some dense greenery Wrance lit a fire. He sat opposite Yfrey, looking at the intense teenager that was now before him. This morning she had been nothing but a child in his eyes, but now she was a young woman, capable of such love and compassion, he knew she had a destiny and he wanted to help her find it.

"What does this mean for us?" she asked him at length. "Where can we go? There's no-where for us now."

"Study the book," Wrance said quietly. "It will lead you to where you need to be. There is a reason it was entrusted into your keeping."

Chapter Thirty-One

"My God Jacques, what have you done to yourself?" Maggie stared in horror at the raised, red area on the back of her daughter's neck.

"It's called a tattoo," Jacques did not turn around from the bathroom mirror, where she was applying black lipstick to her white painted face. "And, I didn't do it myself, Kyle at the tat place did it. I'm going back next week to have him put some ivy growing up my arm. I want to look like a forest."

"Jacques, I think you need to talk to someone."

"I'm talking to you, aren't you enjoying our chat?"

"Someone professional."

"Come on, Mum, hairdressing is a profession, don't put yourself down."

"Jacques, you can't keep doing this, it isn't healthy."

"Doing what?"

"Shutting us all out. You're losing your grip on reality." She paused awkwardly, "I know it's been hard..."

"What? What do you know?" For the first time Jacques turned to face her mother. "Were you the one who had all control taken away? Left bleeding in an alley? Were you the one who had to sit in the witness box whilst that lawyer called you a liar? Can you tell me how hard that was? Because I'd love to know!"

"Of course not, but I've been talking to your father, and we think that you should talk to someone."

"You've been talking about me? Great! What have you been saying? That I'm crazy? Delusional? Perhaps you feel I've lost some of my pep?"

"Jacques, please... this is Doctor Knight, I'd like you to talk to her."

A smartly dressed prim looking woman stepped past the doorway and into view.

"Hello Jacqueline."

"Piss off."

"I understand your hostility towards authority figures, but your parents are concerned about you."

"What do you want?"

"Your parents think it might be best if you come and spend a few weeks at my facility. It's safe, and surrounded by beautiful countryside. We could spend some time talking, and getting to know one another, and hopefully you would feel more positive at the end of it."

"No!" suddenly she was afraid. "Mum, can't you see what's happening? She's one of them! If you let her take me I'll never get out! They want me dead!"

"Jacques, no-one wants you dead. We approached Doctor Knight, we think you need help."

"You didn't mention she was paranoid… when did this start?" Doctor Knight asked Maggie.

"After the attack she took up with some woman. The woman was mad and arrested for murdering a priest. At first we thought Jacques was just trying to defend her, but it has become clear now that Jacques genuinely believes that the priest meant to do her harm, and that this woman was defending her. We are afraid she's been brainwashed, that's part of the reason we called you."

"Don't talk about me like I'm not here!" Jacques screamed. "I'm not delusional! She saved me from that man and she saved me again from that crazy priest! Then she pleaded guilty to save me from having to testify! She is my friend! I'm not crazy!"

"Alright Jacqueline," Doctor Knight's tone never seemed to alter. "Why do you think a priest would want to hurt you?"

"I don't know, but he had some sort of weird dust he kept throwing at me, and a massive knife with a jagged blade."

"They didn't find a knife." Maggie explained, almost in tears.

"I'm not crazy! You know I'm not! Mum, don't do this…"

"Jacques, it's for your own good."

“I won’t go! I’ll fight you! I won’t go!” Jacques grabbed the scissors from the bathroom cabinet and waved them wildly.

“Alright, calm down…” Doctor Knight turned as if to leave, and nodded down the stairs. There was the sound of heavy footsteps ascending towards them.

Jacques made a dash for it, but was grabbed by two large men. She felt a sharp prick in the back of her neck and then the world began to spin, and everything went black.

* * *

“It’s like I can’t go outside, I can’t see my friends, I can’t be normal anymore, because I’m not normal, you know?” Jacques lay on the sofa in Doctor Knight’s office, staring up at the ceiling. “I used to worry about test scores, and whether my nail polish chipped before I was going out. Now I worry that someone might try and touch me, or that I might accidentally do something to make them think it’s OK to touch me. I’m not sure it’ll ever be OK for someone to touch me again.”

“It’s alright to have feelings. That you are now able to articulate them just shows how far you’ve come. People can tell you that it isn’t your fault, that you did nothing wrong, but until you allow yourself to believe it then that man has won. We are making excellent progress here, soon I think you will be able to have visitors.”

“I don’t want visitors.”

“Your brother calls every week, asking if he can see you.”

“I don’t want visitors.”

“Alright then, same time tomorrow?”

“Thanks Doc.”

Jacques returned to her little room down the sparse, clinical corridor. There was a beautiful view of the grounds from her window, but she never looked out. She sat on the bed for hours on end staring at a mark on the wall. What had happened had seemed so real, she had totally believed it. But Doctor Knight had convinced her that a priest had not tried to kill her, it was a paranoid delusion created as a result of a brutal attack for which she had not been counselled early enough, so her brain had sent her into a state of paranoia as a defence mechanism. This all sounded incredibly plausible, but so had her paranoia, at the time. Now, looking back she felt embarrassed, and confused. It had been so real for her. Her parents had spared no expense with her care, clearly relieved that they no longer had to deal with her themselves. As she watched the mark on the wall it seemed to dance and change shape, telling a story in a language that she did not understand. She felt certain that were she to stare at it for long enough then eventually she would know what it was trying to tell her.

Daily she took pills in three colours, and this made the world seem somehow unreal. It was like she was living in some magical dream world, and somewhere, just over the horizon there was a place where no-one could touch her, and she could be free.

"Is she on drugs?" Ben asked as he observed the motionless persona of his sister, staring at the wall.

"Three colours a day!" Jacques turned from her adventure. "I told them I didn't want to see anyone."

"Well, it's been six months, I wanted to see you."

"And am I everything you expected?"

"Jacques…"

"What? What do you want?"

"I want to talk to you about getting out of here."

"I can't get out of here, there is no-where for me to go. Mum and Dad can't even look at me."

"They're having a tough time too. They aren't handling this very well, I know that. I've spoken to some people at the museum, they have a programme to help rehabilitate people who have had mental health issues, they are prepared to interview you for a job in the archives department on a fixed term contract, see how you get on. I can pick you up and take you. Just getting out will help. I think it'll help…" he looked at his feet awkwardly.

"I think it will. Would you wait outside for me? I mean, if I go?"

"Absolutely. I've spoken to the doctor and she thinks that getting out would be good for you."

"You spoke to the doctor before you spoke to me?"

"I wanted to make sure it was alright…"

"I can't go back!" Suddenly she started to shake and her eyes filled with tears. "I can't stand the way they all look at me, like I'm some kind of victim!"

"They don't mean to look at you like that, they don't know what to do, it's been tough on everyone."

"Well, excuse me for not considering everyone else's feelings in this!"

"Jacques, I don't want to argue."

"What do you want? Forgiveness? Don't you get that automatically?"

"I wanted to tell you about this job interview. And about a support group that I've signed you up for. That starts tomorrow. I'll pick you up at six, if you aren't too busy staring at the wall."

"Fine, see you then."

"Alright, see you then."

"Ben?"

"Yes?"

"Thanks for coming."

Chapter Thirty-Two

It had been three years since Yfrey, Wrance and Torius had fled into the forest. Torius had amassed a small but loyal following amongst those who had been driven from their homes, and together they launched guerrilla style raids on neighbouring villages, taking supplies as needed and crippling the resources of any 'Right Way' supporters. They were getting quite a reputation in local communities, and Torius' name was becoming a symbol of hope amongst an increasingly oppressed magical community.

"Torius!" Moki called from his vantage point at the top of a tall tree. "It's Calim himself! He's rounding people up, doing something… I don't know… come look!"

Torius hurried to the base of the tree and scaled it in next to no time, taking the spy glass he peered down into the north-westerly village, predominantly inhabited by magical people, determined not to be driven out. Torius and his people kept a vigil over this village, to protect its inhabitants as best they could.

"Why are they bowing to that pathetic excuse for a man?" Torius exclaimed angrily. "He is two years older than me and even when we were children he was no match for me." He leapt energetically from the tree and seized his sword from inside a hollowed out stump. "I need ten men to come with me now!" he called. "Calim is in the village, it will be the last place he sees!"

Never one for caution, Torius did not stop to assess the situation in the village. Instead he led his men charging into the midst of the village. Calim had been speaking on a podium, and when Torius came running in he stopped, and locked at him calmly.

"Hello, Torius, can I help?"

"You can help the world by dying, you parasite!" Torius leapt on the podium and stabbed Calim in the chest.

As the sword was pulled out Calim laughed good-naturedly. There was no blood, no injury, just a tear in his shirt.

"Oh, Torius, you still think you can solve any problem with violence. You can't kill me, no-one in this world can kill me."

"You cast a spell!" Torius was outraged. "You persecute us and call us unnatural, and you cast a spell to protect yourself. You are an evil hypocrite!"

"Of course I didn't cast a spell; I have no power as you were always wont to remind me. I am blessed, a natural leader for these people. Invulnerable, I can show everyone the right way."

"Over my dead body!"

"If you insist." Calim drew his sword and fought Torius. He had no skills with the weapon but Torius could not strike a blow that would cause damage. Out of the corner of his eye he could see his followers losing against the soldiers who had accompanied Calim. He made a split second decision, and leapt from the podium.

"Retreat!" he cried, and made a bolt for it followed by his men.

* * *

Yfrey and Wrance spent their days down by the river. The magical force field they had erected to protect their woodland encampment swept from the river's edge at the north, to the base of the large blue mountain at the south, and deep into the forest on the east and west. They liked to be on the outskirts. Torius' militant ideals did not match with their naturally peaceful constitutions, and whilst they recognised the need for action, his unplanned assaults on what was essentially civilian outposts was not something they wanted to be associated with. Wrance was teaching Yfrey to hone her abilities, helping her connect with the earth and helping her to make sense of the book.

"Here it says that the feargach will be defeated at the hands of a scarred man," Yfrey looked up at Wrance, her eyes full of concern. "Torius is the feargach, isn't he?"

"Yfrey," Wrance spoke quietly. "Remember the prophecies are there for a reason, to guide you and to warn you. You can impact the outcome of future events if you know they're coming, and that isn't due to happen for years, don't worry."

Just then, from deep into the forest they heard a roar of pain.

"Torius!" Yfrey leapt to her feet and ran towards the sound of the cry.

Torius was on all fours in the dirt, emblazoned on his back was the symbol that had burned outside their home. His hair was no longer the bright white of his people, but a dark brown that matched his eyes.

"What have you done?" Yfrey knew that he must have evoked some very dark magic to achieve this.

"They will never see me coming now, I am the ultimate weapon. Invisible to them, with powers they can only dream of."

"Dark powers. It's not safe to use them, you don't know where they came from. They will consume you."

"I will control them, not the other way around."

"Torius…"

"Trust me, I know what I'm doing."

* * *

"What are you doing?" Torius stabbed the ground next to Yfrey with his sword, leaving it standing upright next to her.

"I'm studying the book." She did not look up at her brother. Since his transformation there was something wrong about his appearance, and it frightened her.

"Is it telling you anything interesting?"

"If I understand it properly we should be searching for something called the Roghnaithe, a sort of, chosen one, to help us return the natural order of the world."

"Well, is that about as clear as it gets? I mean, do we know what he looks like? How can we identify him?"

"Apparently, if we find someone called the Conduit, then, they will lead us to the Roghnaithe. Wrance is helping me interpret the prophecies, he understands them."

"Alright, I'll go talk to him. You should take a break, go chat with some of the men, have some fun."

"I'm fine." Yfrey did not like Torius' little band of rebels, they were coarse and violent. They were also very careful around her, as they knew how protective Torius was of his sister.

Torius approached Wrance, who was sitting on a tree stump, whittling a stick.

"We had a good day today, took out a whole battalion!" he greeted him.

"I don't think you should celebrate all this killing," Wrance spoke without looking up. "It can't possibly end well."

"Yfrey was saying you've been helping her read the book, anything I need to know?"

"If you needed to know anything I would tell you."

"Are you telling Yfrey anything?"

"What she needs to know, and what she is ready to accept."

"You're as vague as that book," Torius rolled his eyes and turned to leave.

"Torius," Wrance called after him. "Take care of your sister, she's important, you know?"

"Why do you think I'm doing this? No-one is going to touch her."

"Just don't lose sight of things."

A noise cut their conversation short.

"It's the warning spell! Get Yfrey and get her out of here, I'll find you when it's safe!" Torius ran towards the sound of the noise.

Wrance hurried to where Yfrey was always sitting, alone, with the book.

"Yfrey, let's go, it's not safe for you here," he called, but he was too late. An inquisitor had her by the hair. She screamed.

"Let her go…" Wrance stopped his approach so as not to provoke the man into any hasty decisions.

"And why would I do that? She is just the leverage we need to trap this rebel. Everyone knows she's his weak link. He should really cut her off."

"You know I won't do that." Torius jammed his blade into the inquisitor's back. "Let her go and I'll let you live."

"And what guarantee do I have of that?"

"My word," Torius looked over at Wrance. "I thought I told you to get her out of here, Wrance?"

"I'm sorry, I wasn't soon enough."

"It wasn't his fault," Yfrey struggled, but to no avail.

“Let her go, now. Last warning.”

“I don’t find you terribly convincing.” The inquisitor tightened his grip of Yfrey.

“Let me see what I can do about that,” Torius moved very close and spoke softly into the man’s ear. Almost at the same time he spoke the man relinquished his grip on Yfrey. She turned quickly to face her attacker. He had fallen to his knees. Torius pulled a small blade from his back and wiped it on his sleeve.

“Torius, what have you done?” Yfrey was trembling, she’d never seen anyone being killed before.

“Exactly what he would have done to you given the chance. You have to toughen up, I can’t keep protecting you like this.” He put the knife back in his belt.

“I never wanted you to protect me like that,” Yfrey couldn’t stop shaking.

“Torius! They’re retreating!” a voice called from further away.

“Get after them!” he responded, drawing his sword. “They know where we are!” He started to run.

“You two stay here, I’ll be back as soon as I can!” he called behind him.

Yfrey stared at the dead body that was lying, face down in the mud at her feet.

“Should we bury him?” she asked Wrance uncertainly.

“It would be respectful,” Wrance observed. “But we don’t have any tools.”

“We can’t just leave him lying there.”

“I’ll go see what I can find. You keep an eye out, and be careful while I’m gone.”

Yfrey sat in the mud with her back against a large oak tree. She willed herself to blend into its bark and make herself invisible. Taking out her knife she looked at it, she could not imagine plunging it into flesh. At length she found herself staring at the body that was lying in the mud in front of her. She wanted the earth to swallow it. She visualised it sinking into the mud and disappearing.

“Yfrey!” Wrance called in a panicked voice. “Yfrey?”

“What? What is it?” Yfrey stood up and hurried towards the worried looking man.

“Where did you come from?”

"I was sitting right there; couldn't you see me?"

"No," Wrance still looked concerned as he handed her a shovel. "Where's the body?"

"Wrance..." Yfrey looked from him, to the ground then back to him. "I think I did it. I don't know how, but I think I did it."

"Did what?"

"I wanted to be invisible against the tree, and I was. I wanted the body eaten by the ground, and it was. I don't know how I did it."

"You have more power than you could possibly know. More than your brother could even imagine. You're beginning to learn to control it. Soon you'll be quite formidable."

"I don't want to be formidable. I don't want to hurt people. We should tell Torius about this."

"No. Your brother's mission is on a small, immediate area. You need to centre your energies on the bigger picture. Focus on studying the book. When the time is right you'll know what to do."

"How do you always know what to do?"

Wrance laughed at this. "Me? I'm just making this up. The trick is to speak with great authority. When you get to my age people assume it's life experience and wisdom."

"Oh, you do know things, you're teasing me."

"Maybe a little bit. Shall we look at the book for a while?"

"Alright then."

Chapter Thirty-Three

The force of the blast sent Verm crashing heavily to the ground. In front of him he could see the remains of what was the toy horse he had carved. He felt a surge of pain and anger flood through his body as he struggled to his feet.

"Yfrey!" he called as he stumbled back towards the wreckage of the building. "Yfrey? Jacques?"

"Your witch is gone!" Calim sneered, stepping out in front of him, sword drawn.

"That may or may not be true," Verm drew his weapon shakily. He was wounded from the explosion and not really in a position to fight. "But you should not have come here, if you think I have even the slightest qualm about ending you, then you'd be wrong."

"I don't fear you." Calim was small, and seemed to be struggling to hold the sword, yet his arrogance was undeniable. "The only person who could kill me has been blown up in that building, now I am indestructible."

"Care to put that to the test?" Verm raised his sword.

"You foolish man! Can't you see that you have played into my hands this whole journey? I know, don't you see? I knew all along! I could not kill the Roghnaithe in her own world, but I had to make it look like you idiots had the idea to bring her here. Then I let the seer think it was his idea to bring the witch, I knew the guilt would make him turn and help you. I knew everything!"

"You talk too much!" Verm swung his sword hard and Calim dodged and thrust a counter blow. Blocking a downward strike he drew a small dagger and slashed Verm's sword arm causing him to drop his sword. Before he was able to regroup, Calim kicked him to the ground and stood over him with the sword. As he went to strike the fatal blow Torius leapt in the way of the blade, ending up with the sword squarely through his chest.

“Not quite what I had in mind,” Calim said, as he pulled the weapon free. “But it’ll do.”

Torius looked down at where the weapon had entered. He was not even bleeding.

“It’ll take more than a sword, Calim. Didn’t see that coming, did you?”

“What is this?” Calim stepped back in fear.

“Curious thing about magic, if you use it to mess with the natural order of things it’ll find a way to come back and bite you. You can’t be killed. If someone comes at you with the intention of killing you then you are impervious, but if the intention is to keep you alive as long as possible whilst torturing you, well, that’ll work out just fine, wanna see?” Torius drew his sword and advanced on Calim.

Calim awkwardly fended off the attack.

“Typical Torius, putting revenge before your sister’s life. All the time you’re fighting me she’s probably dying in the rubble.” This statement made Torius hesitate long enough for Calim to turn tail and run.

“Damn coward!” Torius stabbed the ground angrily with his sword once he realised the deception. He turned to Verm and offered him his hand. “You should get that arm looked at,” he ripped the sleeve from his shirt and wound it tightly around Verm’s arm to stop the bleeding.

“I will when the area is secure. It looks like we won the day, if you can call this a win.”

The battle seemed to be over; Calim’s troops were retreating and the rebels were looking to the two men for further guidance.

“Was he telling the truth about Yfrey? Was she still in the building?”

“I didn’t see her come out.”

“Then we have to find her.” Torius stumbled over the wreckage to the blast site and started to throw rubble around in a desperate search attempt.

Verm was feeling dizzy. Using his sword as a walking aid, he struggled towards one of his captains.

“We need to secure the area,” he spoke authoritatively. “See if we can commandeer a civilian residence to treat the wounded. Set up camp centrally and take as many men as you need to turn that rubble into barricades on the road. I want to limit points of access. We are very vulnerable at the moment, we haven't won this thing yet."

The soldier nodded and left without saying a word. Verm's dizziness finally got the better of him and he passed out on the ground.

When he came to, he was in what appeared to be a makeshift command tent. His wounds had been cleaned and dressed and he was alone. From outside he heard voices.

"The general is resting; he should not be disturbed."

"Would it disturb him if I killed you?"

"It's alright, let him in," Verm called. He felt very glad that someone had left the bottle of alcohol that had been used to sterilise his wounds. He took a large swig.

"She's not there!" Torius said, barging in.

"Who's not where?" Verm's head hurt.

"Yfrey, she's not in the rubble. She must have escaped somehow."

"She's very resourceful. Perhaps immortality is a family trait?"

"I'm not immortal."

"Well, you took that sword to the chest very well."

"Calim cast a spell which says that no-one of this world can kill him. That's why all the prophecies point to Jacques. All I did was piggyback off his spell. I am his equal and opposite reaction. As long as he exists I exist. I will always be there to oppose him."

"And when Jacques kills him?"

"My work will be done."

"So, why don't we just kill you? Or get Jacques to kill you?"

"It doesn't work like that. I'm tied to him, not the other way around."

"But you aren't invulnerable. I mean, I was able to hurt you."

"He isn't invulnerable, we can both be hurt. It is only if the intention is to kill that the act fails. You see, magic is designed to preserve the natural order, not destroy it. Everything has consequences. The consequence for Calim is that as long as we don't intend to kill him he can live forever in infinite agony."

Verm scratched his head. He did not like the look of glee that was in Torius' eyes as he envisioned the torture of another human being. Nor did he like the fact that Torius was unkillable. He had always comforted himself that if Torius ever became too much to handle he would simply end him. With this option off the table he would need to rethink.

"Can't the spell be broken?" he asked, carefully moderating his tone.

"All spells can be broken," Torius clearly felt that they were still discussing Calim. "Why do you think he has led an attack on the magical community? Keeps us on the move and eliminates any potential threats. We need someone powerful to understand the spell and reverse it; way more powerful than me."

"You cast a spell without fully understanding what it was."

"Yes, I was angry and afraid. The darker powers are easier to channel when you feel strong negative emotions."

"We need Yfrey." Verm spoke definitely.

"On that we agree, but I wouldn't know where to begin."

"I would, there is a tracker tied to a tree about a day's ride from the top of the mountain. Our horses are tethered at the top. Take whatever men you need."

"I won't need any men." And with that, Torius was gone.

Verm sighed. He needed a plan. He needed to fortify their current position and come up with a plan to gain ground. He needed to get some sort of holding cell for Calim, if they defeated him before they found Jacques then he would need to be contained. But most of all he needed Yfrey. He could not remember how he had been able to function or make decisions before he had known her. It was ridiculous. He was an army general. The decisions he made affected the very lives of the men under his command, and yet, now Yfrey was gone, he felt this gaping emptiness in his very soul. He could not explain or quantify the feeling. He just knew that he needed her back. Sighing he took another swig of alcohol. He needed to think.

Chapter Thirty-Four

"Are dragons usually friendly?" Yfrey stared at the massive red lizard that was flying towards them from above the mountain.

"Not according to legend, no…"

"Do you think perhaps we should run then?"

"Might be an idea…" Jacques did not move, still staring at the creature.

"Jacques?"

"Yes?"

"You aren't moving."

"No…"

"I think that perhaps you should…"

"Right, yeah." Taking Yfrey's hand she turned and they both started to run. There was a dense forest up ahead and it was their hope that the movements of such a vast creature would be hampered by a close proximity to trees.

Suddenly the ground started to tremble beneath them and what seemed like an army of horses came thundering out of the trees.

"Oh, bloody hell! Not horses!" Jacques pulled Yfrey out of the way as the two of them tumbled to the ground in their haste to avoid the oncoming army. Atop the beasts were knights in armour, all ascending at a pace towards the dragon, which flapped and hovered above them as they bombarded it with sticks and spears. Wounded, the creature plummeted to the earth and the men dismounted and moved in for the kill.

"Alright, that's enough." Jacques stood up and made her way purposefully towards the crowd.

"Jacques! What are you doing?" Yfrey hurried after her.

"They are bullying that dragon and I don't like it."

"You don't know the circumstances!" Yfrey objected strenuously as Jacques moved in on the group of men.

"I know enough to see that this isn't a fair fight!" Jacques spoke loudly as she approached the group that surrounded the dragon. "Hey! Back off that dragon!"

The men stopped and looked at her. One, seemingly the leader, spoke.

"Who are you?"

"Well, I'm glad you asked," Jacques began awkwardly. She really had not thought this through at all. "I am from The Society For The Ethical Treatment Of Dragons, and before I let you continue here, I need you to justify your actions, um, please."

"Ha! What a strange little woman you are, with your bi coloured hair and strange markings. There is no such society. When we slay the dragon we can sell its parts for relics and return as heroes. Now, run along home."

"OK, so, a couple of things: first, it's been a while since I've been to the chemist, so my roots are starting to show, and actually it is quite rude of you to comment. Second, my tattoos are not strange markings, they are body art, and three, you are not going to touch that dragon."

She drew her dagger from her belt and watched as it grew into a full length glistening sword. The men all took a step back in amazement at what they had just witnessed. One drew his sword and stepped forward. Suddenly the others followed suit and Jacques found herself in the middle of a battle. Her sword seemed to take on a life of its own and fought for her, anticipating her thoughts and moving on command. Still, there were many of them and only one of her.

"Evie! A little help here?" she called as she fought.

Yfrey sighed. She did not know what use she could be here. She reached into her pocket and drew her knife. Except it was not her knife. It was much lighter. It was a stick. Her knife had been replaced by a stick.

"Seriously?" Yfrey spoke to the sky. "She gets a sword and I get a stick?" She shook it hard hoping it would turn back into a blade. Some sort of charge emanated from it and suddenly the army had no weapons and no armour. They looked at one another for a moment before the man who had spoken to Jacques bellowed:

"Retreat!"

They retreated to their horses and rode away. Jacques' sword turned back into a knife and she sheathed it in her belt.

"What the hell just happened?" she demanded.

"I think my stick did it…" Yfrey looked the piece of wood in her hand.

"Your stick?" Jacques stared at her incredulously. "Where did you find the stick?"

"It was where my knife used to be."

"Well, clearly it's a magic stick, so keep hold of it. I can't believe I just said that." Jacques moved tentatively towards the dragon, holding her hand out for it to sniff. "Easy, Buddy, it's alright." It had a spear sticking out of its side and a number of gashes from the assault. "We're gonna have to get this spear out, but I don't know how."

"You don't even like horses, and you want a pet dragon?" Yfrey demanded.

"No, I don't want a pet dragon, I just want it to have a fighting chance if those men come back."

"Alright, let's see if I can do it with my stick." Yfrey offered.

"Sure, let's see what your stick can do." Jacques said sarcastically.

Choosing to ignore the tone, Yfrey held her stick in both hands and imagined it dissolving the spear into the air and healing the dragon's wounds. When she opened her eyes the spear was gone and the dragon was on its feet looking at them.

"It worked!" Yfrey was amazed.

"It worked." Jacques grinned broadly. "I think your stick might be a magic wand."

Yfrey shrugged and looked at the dragon.

"Thank you." Its voice was deep and booming but surprisingly gentle.

"Oh shit!" Jacques took a step backwards.

"What?" Yfrey and the dragon spoke simultaneously.

"I don't know, I guess I just didn't expect you to be able to talk," Jacques began awkwardly.

"Dragon's only talk when we have something important to say," the creature boomed.

"Well, um, you're welcome. Do you know where we can go that's away from those men?"

"Climb on my back, I will take you to the island of dragons, you will be safe with us."

Tentatively they climbed on the dragon's back. The air around them made a loud booming noise as its wings beat against it. Soon they were high above this new world, looking down on fields, woods, mountains, rivers, lakes, small villages and one very dark, ominous looking castle.

"What's that?" Jacques asked, as they flew over at great speed.

"That is a very dark and dangerous place," the dragon boomed. "You must stay away from there."

Soon it was out of site and they were flying above an ocean, on their way to Dragon Island.

"So, I know this is kind of an afterthought, but you aren't going to eat us when we land?"

In all the excitement and adventure of the moment Jacques had forgotten that the dragons of legend eat people.

"Dragons are herbivores," the dragon informed her.

"Wow, the legends really got it wrong. I suppose you don't breathe fire either?"

"We can breathe fire, but it takes a lot out of us, and sometimes the effect of the flames causes our throats to close over. Dragons have been known to die of suffocation after attempting it. It is often a mother's last attempt to defend her nest."

"Tragic..." Jacques felt a deep pang of sadness for these misunderstood creatures.

"What do your legends say?" Yfrey asked. Until now she had been sitting quietly watching the world fly by beneath them.

"Oh, there's lots of stuff about dragons murdering people, burning villages, killing children, then brave knights would come along and kill them. Our Patron Saint, St George is famous for slaying a dragon."

"I suppose it would have been less impressive if the legend said that the dragon ate leaves and lived peacefully." Yfrey observed, then added, "Even with that knowledge, you still risked yourself for a dragon."

"Well, I didn't really think about it until now. I just don't like bullies, never have."

"That's because you're a hero."

"Well, I wouldn't go that far."

"I know, that's why you are."

Chapter Thirty-Five

"We're under attack!" A cry from outside was accompanied by gun fire. Verm dropped his bottle, grabbed his sword and hurried to the sound of the cry.

"Where's the attack coming from?" he demanded of anyone who would listen.

"Over there, by the south-west border," called a man with a rifle, who was hurrying towards the noise. Verm matched his pace and joined him.

"We need to fortify!" he called, storming past people who seemed at a loss as to what to do. "Help build a barricade; they'll exploit any weakness!"

An upturned market stall served as the only protection to the men who were attempting to defend the city. They were not soldiers and had no weapons. Several had already been shot and were lying on the ground. The man running next to Verm started to shoot over the stall as he ran. Verm grabbed his arm and pulled him to the ground so that the two men were sitting with their backs to the upturned market stall.

"Don't waste bullets!" he said firmly to the man, who was breathing heavily. "On my mark, you cover me, do you understand?"

The man nodded. He leapt over the stall and raced with his sword drawn towards the attackers. The men did not know what had hit them, and within seconds they were all dead.

"Come here and collect their weapons, we need them," he commanded the men who were still able to move. "Build a barricade, requisition what you need. They are not getting through here. And someone find me a MEDIC!"

Some men came running towards him carrying stretcher boards.

"We've got no-where to bring the wounded, Sir," one of the men looked to Verm for direction.

"Well, where did the wounded go when people just lived here?" Verm had no idea what he was doing and he hated it.

"Central Hospital was closed over a year ago, Calim said that treating the sick and the weak was a waste of government resources, and the people couldn't afford to keep it open and pay their taxes."

"Well, what happened to all the medics?"

"They left, or took menial jobs."

"Right, get these people to the old building, get it open and see if there are any supplies you can salvage. I'll see about getting us a medic."

He strode purposefully through the rubble. People were making themselves busy trying to erect a barricade, but at the sight of Verm they stopped and watched him respectfully.

"Do any of you have medical training?"

"I do," a man in a cleaner's uniform stepped forward.

"I'm reopening the hospital; can you help?"

"I used to run it."

Verm looked at this undernourished man in his grubby overalls – such skill and training, totally wasted.

"What are you going to need to get it up and running again?"

"A staff, a through route to the hospital for supplies, we can't run it on air."

"Do what you can with what's available here, I'll see what else I can get you, but we'll need to fortify as a priority, a through route will make us vulnerable at this point."

"I understand."

"Messenger!" Verm bellowed. A slim youth answered his cry. "I need you to get to any battalions that are within range and get their allegiance, we can't just bury ourselves in here, we'll rot. Tell them that Verm says the time to act has come. They'll know what that means. Keep safe."

"Yes, Sir."

* * *

Borana bolted upright in bed. The sound of her own scream had woken her. Portan hurried in to see what was wrong, her scream had woken him also. He entered her room to find her sitting up in bed sweating profusely and trembling.

"What is it? What's wrong?"

"They're coming for us."

"Who?"

"The soldiers. Verm is soon to secure victory and they know that you are his weakness."

"Then we should run, let's pack some things."

"We can't, I need to build another portal. I have to start now if it's going to be ready in time."

"In time for what?"

"To bring Jacques and Yfrey back for the final battle."

"What do you need?"

Chapter Thirty-Six

Dragon Island was lush and green, unspoilt by any interaction with humans and their constant need to build and progress. As they alighted on the ground, Jacques and Yfrey found themselves surrounded by the giant flying lizards, all in a variety of bright colours.

"You brought these vermin here?" one demanded of their dragon. "They hunt and kill us, ravage and mutilate the land and you bring them here? Are you out of your mind?"

"They are not like the others, they saved me from an attack."

The big dragon leaned down and sniffed them suspiciously.

"They aren't from here," it observed.

"Perhaps they're like the other strangers, sent here by strange forces?" another offered.

"Others?" Yfrey asked.

"They smell the same as you," their dragon informed her. "They fall from the sky and are gathered up by the men on horses and taken to the dark castle."

"This one smells different again," added another dragon as it sniffed Jacques.

"Hey! Quit sniffing me, it isn't polite!"

"They saved me and they will have our hospitality as long as they require it."

The dragons seemed to have lost interest in them as this last statement was being spoken and had begun to disperse.

"Hey, thanks." Jacques smiled at the great creature as it towered above her. "What's your name anyway?"

"We do not have names. We each know who we are and have no need to assign labels."

"But how do you know who you're talking to?"

"We just do."

“Hmmm. I need to think. Is it safe to walk here?”
“You're safe.”
“Thanks.”

* * *

“What do you know about the castle?” Yfrey asked thoughtfully. It was dusk and she was sitting on a tree branch to allow herself to be eye level with the dragon.

“I think it is a prison. We avoid it as there is a dark power emanating from it. It is not naturally of this world. It has been manipulated somehow. It's evil, for want of a better word. I don't really know what it means, but it's a word that seems to suit that place.”

“Calim has found some way to manipulate your world and ours. At first I thought he didn't like magic because he had none, so resented it. Now I see that he wants to be the only one with magic, so there is no threat to his power.”

“No-one dares go near that castle,” the dragon spoke softly. “You shouldn't until you know more about it, it's a dangerous place.”

“I should consult the book,” Yfrey spoke more to herself than to her companion now. She reached into her inside pocket to retrieve The Book of Abisan. “It's not here!” she started to panic as she groped around in the pocket hoping that she had missed it. “It must have fallen out in the explosion.” She could feel herself breaking into a cold sweat as she continued desperately to feel around in her pocket. Her hand touched on a small metal object. Quickly she pulled it out and examined it. It was a pendant on a chain. The black stone was encased in a metal frame, which had carved into it the same markings that had been on the top of the book.

“Everything's different here,” she said quietly as she held the pendant out in front of her. Before her eyes it began to spin quickly and a vision began to appear. She saw the dark castle flickering in the night air. Her view moved closer and she was inside. She saw people like her, magical beings. They were not chained or restrained in any way, but they were immobile. All staring straight in front of them at some invisible mesmerising force. The image dispersed.

“I have to find Jacques,” she said as she leapt out of the branch and into the soft grass below. “I know where the prisoners are.”

“She headed towards the beach,” the dragon indicated a direction with its giant head. Yfrey hurried away.

Jacques was sitting on the sand staring at the waves. She did not hear Yfrey approach.

“We have to go to that scary castle,” Yfrey informed her, as she seated herself next to Jacques on the sand.

“Wait, what? Why?”

“That's where the prisoners are.”

“How do you know?”

“The book told me.”

“It didn't tell you before now...” Jacques was dubious.

“Well, it wasn't a pendant before now.”

“What?” Jacques sighed. “Start at the beginning.”

Yfrey explained what she had seen and Jacques listened carefully.

“So why don't they just leave if they aren't restrained at all?” she asked when Yfrey had finished.

“Because they are under some sort of spell.”

“And how do you know that the exact same thing won't happen to us when we set foot in there?”

“Well, I don't. But we have to do something, we can't just leave them there.”

“I agree, but we can't just go in half cocked either. That hasn't worked out so well for us so far.”

“We're still alive.”

“Barely. And I've been shot, slashed, punched and blown up. I'd like a scenario that doesn't result in me being injured if at all possible.”

“So, what would you suggest?”

“I don't know, you're the ideas girl, can't you ask your pendant?”

“I suppose I could.” Yfrey took it from around her neck and held it out in front of her. It began to spin again. This time, however, the blurry image began to form much bigger, it seemed to surround them. In front of them they saw the large black building looming ominously. As Jacques looked down she realised that she was now sitting on grass.

“Brilliant. I guess your book has spoken. I liked it better when it contained vague prophecies and hints. This is a bit too proactive for me.”

“What do we do now?” Yfrey asked, as she replaced the pendant around her neck and reached out her hand to touch the dark stone wall that formed the side of the castle. “Dark magic surrounds this place.”

“Don't need to be a witch to see that. I guess we try and find a way in, come on.” Jacques moved close to the wall, examining it for any sign of weakness.

“Maybe my stick could help?”

Yfrey took the wand from her pocket and held it in both hands. She visualised them both being inside the dark walls. Suddenly she was alone in a dark room. “Éadrom!” she spoke loudly clapping her hands twice. A soft light illuminated the room. She could hear voices in the distance, shouting, as though a battle was raging, but she couldn't see anything, she tried to go towards the noise, but it was all around, and yet nowhere all at once. “Jacques?” she called into the distant darkness, but there was no response.

Chapter Thirty-Seven

Verm requisitioned a land craft to get back to his father's home as soon as possible. He needed to speak to someone magical that he could trust and he knew that Borana would still be there. He banged heavily on the door and called out.

"What are you doing here?" Portan asked as he scanned the perimeter nervously. "Did you come in that?"

"Yes, I did. Are you alright?"

"At least now we know how they find us." Borana said, looking up from the table.

"What? Who?" Verm was confused.

"It's alright, they're supposed to find us. What do you need?" Portan asked calmly.

"I need to talk to her, I need a seer."

"What do you want to know?"

"I need to know how to stop Torius, if I have to, and Calim. If Jacques doesn't come back, I'll need a plan. I don't have prison facilities and my resources are limited."

"I can't help you with this, but I can send you to someone who can. It's in another reality. You'll need help to fit in. The only way I think you'll be able to get to her is to work within their system. It'll be difficult."

"I'm ready, show me what to do."

"I knew you would ask me to do this, so I have prepared some supplies," Borana opened the drawer and pulled out a number of glass bottles filled with what appeared to be coloured gas. "I have contained portals within these bottles, they are fortified by magic. Break the glass by throwing it hard against a stationary object, a portal will form wherever it hits. It will remain open for ten-seconds, so time it carefully. The blue will take you where you need to be, the red will take you home."

“What does the green do?”

“You must only use the green in emergencies, it will do what you need.”

“You magical people are so vague.”

“It's part of our allure. You won't be able to fight your way to what you need once you're through the portal, it's a different world.”

“I will have to rely on my wits and charm.”

“Um, yeah, about that...”

“What?” Verm raised an eyebrow in mock affront.

“Well, this world has natural magic, which means we can understand each other no matter what province we are from. Magical beings carry this ability with them when they travel inter-dimensionally. You are not a magical being.”

“So what are you saying? I won't be able to understand anyone when I get there?”

“I'm saying you will need to wear this.” Borana held out a jewelled cross pendant. “I stole it from that soldier who had a hold of me in the tavern.”

“I am not wearing that,” Verm said firmly. “I find everything it represent abhorrent.”

“You'll have to. You won't be able to achieve your mission without it. Calim has been sending men through to that world for years now, and I managed to find out how. The stones in this pendant have been blessed by someone with very powerful magic, much more powerful than I have ever seen. I could never do it.”

“Fine.” Verm put the chain around his neck. As he pushed his hair out of his face Borana noticed a white stripe of hair behind his right ear. The magic had begun to take effect.

“When you are ready, throw the bottle against the wall and step through the portal. Remember it will close after ten-seconds to prevent you from being followed, or at least it should.”

“What does that mean?”

“Well, this is a new way of creating portals, and it means you won't leave a magical trail behind you...”

“But?”

“But I've only just invented it, and it hasn't been tested yet. It should work,” she offered reassuringly.

“Great, that makes me feel so much better.” Verm threw the blue bottle against the wall, and before his eyes the world seemed to turn to liquid. Uncertainly he stepped through and the portal closed behind him.

“Do-do-do-do-don't move,” stammered a little man holding a small black handled knife. From the state of the blade Verm would have guessed that he had been using it to eat prior to adopting it as a weapon.

Verm sized this strange little man up. He had black spectacles and a multi-coloured shirt that looked like it would not withstand even a day of manual labour. His trousers matched his shirt and on his feet he wore what appeared to be synthetic animal heads. Verm quickly decided that this man was no threat.

“Where am I?” he demanded.

“You don't know?”

“Not exactly, no.”

“Well, you've wasted your time, anyway. She's somewhere you will never be able to get to her.”

“Who?”

“What?”

“Alright, you strange little man, I don't know who you think I am, but whoever it is, it's not me. Now, unless you plan to eat fruit just put that blade down and tell me what's going on.”

“You don't want to kill her?”

“Who?”

“Carys.”

“Karus.” Verm spat the name out as the indelible mark she had left on his face meant she would always be with him. “So, that's why I'm here. Where is she?”

“What do you want with her?”

“I want her to help me with a project.”

The man looked dubiously at Verm. He was still pointing the knife at him.

“How do I know you won't hurt her?”

"You don't. And I can't promise she won't be hurt, but it won't be at my hand. I do know that she came here with a mission, and I can help her with that, but you'll have to tell me where she is."

"She's in prison." The man sighed, lowered his knife and indicated that Verm should move into to next room. The room seemed warm and comfortable. There was a strange unnatural light emanating from the walls, which would have been harsh and bright had it not been for the tinted glass that shaded it. The man indicated that Verm should sit on one of the tall wooden chairs that surrounded a round wooden table, which was strewn with papers.

"What's this?" Verm asked. The papers contained strange symbols that he neither recognised nor understood.

"It's Carys' case," the man looked awkward. "I've been working to get her out for over ten years. The evidence was irrefutable, but I know her, she wouldn't, couldn't have done what they said she did."

"Can we get her out by force?" Verm asked. He had never been one for red tape. "What is the security like where she is?"

"We can't break her out. They won't even let anyone in to see her, say she's too dangerous. She refused to see me, or a solicitor, it's like she wants to rot in there."

"What's a solicitor?"

"A representative. Her only hope of getting out."

"Can I do that?"

"Do you know anything about the law?"

"No – can I bluff it?"

"Maybe... I have a couple of DVDs you could watch, and you'd need a suit. Why would they send someone to help after all this time?"

"I was hoping she could help me, if I need to help her first then I will." Verm said honestly. "If you can get me in then I can get her out. Show me these DVDs of which you speak."

Chapter Thirty-Eight

Suddenly Yfrey was back in her world. Everything was very hectic, there were people shouting and hurrying to and fro. She seemed to be at the base of what used to be the dark tower, but there was no sign of it, instead the bricks appeared to have been used to build a wall which surrounded some tents. She heard a bang and something hit her. She was face down in the rubble and someone was on top of her.

“What are you doing just standing around?” Torius hissed in her ear. “Can't you see we're under siege?” he rolled off her and grabbed her wrist. “Stay low and keep close to me,” he instructed.

“What's going on, where's Jacques?”

“She's around, don't worry, she can take care of herself.”

“We shouldn't be here. I mean, we weren't here, this isn't right.” Yfrey cried as she was dragged through the mayhem.

“Yfrey, you're making no sense, shut up and stay with me.”

“Verm!” she screamed, seeing Verm under attack by four large armed men.

“Stay here!” Torius drew his sword and rushed into the fray.

Yfrey followed, drawing her knife from her pocket.

“Yfrey! Stay down!” Verm called as he and Torius battled the four assailants.

“What's going on?” Yfrey demanded, slashing with her knife as best she could.

“What do you mean?” Verm asked as he blocked a blow to her head and knocked her attacker unconscious with his fist.

“I wasn't here, I was somewhere else, where's Jacques?”

“You were over there,” Verm informed her between blows. “Now you're here. Jacques is looking for Calim, she knows what she has to do.”

“This isn't right, though!” Yfrey objected.

“War is never right, but in some cases it's necessary. If Jacques is successful it will end today.” With this last statement Verm drew his blade from the stomach of his attacker and wiped it with his glove.

“We should get her somewhere safe,” Torius said, running back towards them, sword in hand. “The way she's acting, it's like she's been hit on the head or something.”

“Agreed. Follow me.” Verm said, leading the way through the chaos that lay before them.

As they moved behind one of the brick barriers Torius cried out in pain and collapsed.

“What happened?” Yfrey turned sharply at the sound of the cry. As she hurried to her brother's side she could see a huge wound across his stomach.

“She's done it!” Torius gasped, a curious smile breaking across his face. “Now she just needs to finish it.”

“Who? Finish what? Verm!”

“It's alright, Yfrey,” Verm put his hand gently on her shoulder. “Your brother died a long time ago. Now Jacques has done her job, at least his pain can end.”

“You tied your life to Calim? That's what you did! I knew you'd done something awful. How could you do this?”

“I had to. I'd been hit with a death dart. Who would have protected you?”

“We should be protecting each other. If you'd spoken to me instead of tapping into dark powers, then we could have found a solution.”

Torius cried out again, he had been slashed to his arm.

“This isn't happening, not today!” Yfrey ran into the crowds searching for Jacques.

“Drop your sword and surrender, you're beaten.” Jacques gasped as she watched Calim struggle to remain standing.

“Not a chance. They summoned you to kill me,” Calim gasped. “And to defeat me that is what you will have to do. I'm dying a martyr, not living a failure.”

“As you like.” Jacques said and scissor kicked him in the chest, so that he lost his footing and fell to the ground.

“Jacques! No!” Yfrey called as she hurried towards her.

For a second Jacques turned to where Yfrey was, and Calim took his opportunity and stabbed her in the stomach. Jacques gasped and grabbed her wound falling backwards.

“Evie,” she breathed quietly.

“No!” Yfrey rushed to her side, tearing the pocket from her cloak she applied pressure to the wound. “You'll be OK, we'll get you to Portan, he'll fix you, you'll be OK.”

Jacques gently put her hand over Yfrey's as she applied pressure to the wound.

“It's too late for that, Evie,” she smiled weakly. “At least I've done what I was needed for.” Her breathing was becoming increasingly laboured as she looked towards Calim, who had clearly used his last strength to inflict the fatal wound upon her.

“No, it's not!” Yfrey said urgently, looking around for someone to help them.

“Evie, it's OK.” Jacques gasped. “How could I have gone home after this? There would have been no place for me. I've done what I needed to, it's over.”

“No! It's not!” Yfrey was almost crying. “Here is a place for you! You can stay with me. Don't go! Don't go! Jacques! Jacques!” Jacques was not breathing. Yfrey was supporting the lifeless body in her arms. She couldn't put it down, as that would make it real. Verm strode past her, picked up Calim's body by the neck and cried in a booming voice across the sea of violence:

“It's over! Lay down your arms!”

Almost immediately an oppressive wave of silence swept over them. Yfrey did not move. How could it be over? This was not how it was supposed to be. Jacques was gone, Torius was gone, she had no-one left, no purpose; there was nothing for her now. She clung to Jacques' body, somehow feeling that if she let go then she would be accepting defeat. Accepting that it was over; that there was nothing she could do.

“Yfrey?” Verm spoke gently to her. “You need to let go now. We'll bury the dead tomorrow. They will all receive proper respect, but right now we must tend to the wounded and see what we can salvage from the skeleton of this city. We need to form a government before everything descends into chaos."

"No." Yfrey said firmly. "This is not how things are meant to be – I will not accept it. This should not be happening. I'm not moving until things get back to how they're supposed to be. I'm not moving!"

"Alright..." Verm said awkwardly. "I'll come back for you when you're ready, I need to take charge now."

"It's not over..." Yfrey muttered to herself, oblivious to anything that was going on around her. Day turned into night but she did not notice. She simply sat alone in the darkness.

Chapter Thirty-Nine

Verm examined himself in the long wall mirror. He looked very dapper in his three-piece suit and shiny black shoes.

"It's not very practical, is it?" he complained as he turned and examined his backside. "Where am I supposed to keep my sword?"

"You can't bring a sword into a prison," Barry explained. "They'll search you. You can't bring anything suspicious in at all. You'll need to get her out legally, or just talk to her in there."

"Alright," Verm said dubiously. "I've watched your DVDs, I think I can convince them of my credentials, but if they ask for proof I have nothing."

"Sure you do," Barry said confidently, handing him a leather wallet with a number of plastic cards in. "These two are credit cards, in case you need to buy anything. The pin is written on the inside flap here. This is your driver's license, Bar Association membership, library card and photo of your kids. You are the Right Honourable Vernon Clemonts, you did your degree at Trinity, and set up a private practice. Hell, the hardest part was finding you that outfit. Who has size eighteen feet?"

"It's a ridiculous outfit," Verm objected pulling his tie. "I feel like I'm being strangled."

"Leave it alone!" Barry scolded. "It's a Windsor knot."

"Feels more like a hangman's knot," Verm grumbled as Barry led him out to his tiny car. "You expect me to get in there?"

"It's very economical and parking is a doddle."

"You would not comfortably fit a child in that!"

"You are so grouchy. Just get in and shut up!"

Barry waited outside in the car as Verm strode purposefully into the prison.

"Vernon Clemonts, solicitor for Carys Sinclair, you're expecting me," he said assertively to the guard.

“No papers or anything?” the guard looked at the ID suspiciously. “Most of you people come with massive briefcases for me to look through.”

“I have a photographic memory,” Verm said. “Would you take me to my client?”

“Sure. You wanna be careful with this one, she killed a priest. Complete psycho if you ask me.”

“I didn't ask you. And I believe that this isn't in fact the case, or I would not be doing this pro-bono, would I?”

“Spose not. Go on through.”

Verm was led down an oppressive corridor to a room which had a heavy metal door.

“It's right in there,” a second guard indicated the door. “I'll wait here, there's no way I'm going anywhere near that psycho.”

Verm pushed the door open. Sitting handcuffed to a chair behind a large table was Karus. She looked tired.

“General Verm. Have you come to kill me?”

“No, I need your help.” Verm seated himself opposite her.

“And what could a lowly citizen like me possibly do for the might of Calim's government?”

“I am no longer with the government. I work with Yfrey to free our people.”

“You always were very vocal against Calim. When I saw that you were still alive I presumed you had changed your allegiance,” she looked at him suspiciously.

“I stayed in service to the army until it was no longer palatable. Yfrey brought hope to our world, I can't remember the last time that I felt I could make a difference. But since I have met Jacques and seen what she is capable of I have expected more of myself.”

“Jacques? Yfrey found her? Does she have the blade?”

“Yes, she wields it masterfully.”

“Barry found a way to get it to her, then. He's a good man.”

“Yes, he seems to be. He is not from our world though.”

“No, I met him when I first arrived here. I couldn't have done anything without him.”

“Why won't you let him see you?”

“I can't. If they thought he was helping me they'd kill him. He's a good, kind, gentle man. He's not accustomed to violence. He wouldn't stand a chance.”

“Who is after you?”

“I don't know. I was attacked by an inquisitor, I defeated him but it was in a very public place. There were witnesses. I could not explain my actions so I remained silent.”

“It's possible I've lost Jacques...” Verm began awkwardly. “I need an alternative. Torius has used dark powers to tie his life to Calim's. I don't know which is the bigger threat to the possibility of peace. I need to get you out, what can I do?”

“You don't need me, you need to talk to Barry. Before they put me in here he was working on something for me. Ask him for it. But Verm, you need to protect him. Promise me.”

“I promise. And I promise that as soon as things are resolved I will get you out of here.”

Verm banged the door with his hand. He was escorted outside where Barry was waiting for him.

“Well?”

“She's fine. She cares for you very much. Said you have what I came for.”

“I do, I have been developing it for years. But you can't have it.”

“Why not?” Verm was cramped in the tiny vehicle and becoming extremely irritated.

“No offence, but I don't know you. I developed it for her, and will give it to her. You get her out and we both get what we want.”

“What do you want?”

“I want my wife out of jail. Now, do we have an understanding?”

“We do. I think I know how to do it. Take me home and I'll explain.”

Chapter Forty

Jacques cursed as she kicked the outside of the black castle, trying to find a weakness in the structure. Yfrey had just vanished and now she was alone in this strange place with untold dangers around her.

"Jacques..." The deep booming tones of the dragon were behind her, but when she turned around she was met by a lean, handsome young man.

"Dragon?"

"Yes. When I saw you carried away on the air stream I thought I ought to follow, to make sure that you were alright."

"Is that what happened? How did you make yourself look like a man?"

"We all have that ability. I thought I would be less obtrusive in this form, at least until we know what we're dealing with."

"Good idea. But, if you can appear like that why don't you just do it all the time? You'd probably be attacked less."

"Why should I hide who I am? I can't fly in this form. Besides, if we all appeared as members of their species, they would start looking for differences in each other to attack, as is their way."

"I get it. I kinda feel the same way. Thanks for coming, you didn't have to."

"You didn't have to leap into a fight where you were vastly outnumbered to defend a creature you didn't know. It is when faced with adversity that we see our true selves, and your true self is worth protecting. I would consider it an honour to be your protector."

"Wow, thanks, Dragon. I'm truly touched. We need to find a way to get in here. I think Evie was sucked in."

The dragon put both hands on the stone wall and closed its eyes. Jacques looked around nervously and fingered the hilt of her sword.

"The door is concealed by dark magic," the dragon eventually spoke. "I will be able to locate it, but I don't think I have the power to open it."

"Don't worry about that," Jacques said confidently, patting her sword. "You find it, I'll smash it open. Hitting the computer at work always made it work, I can't see this being any different." Seeing the dragon's look of confusion, she added; "that was a joke. You find the door, then we'll work out our next move."

Shutting its eyes the dragon put both hands against the dark stone once more and breathed deeply. Then it stepped away and frowned.

"What?" Jacques demanded.

"The entire structure is an illusion," the creature looked at her as though it didn't quite believe what it was saying itself. "It's only keeping us out because we believe it can."

"So, in theory I could walk through the wall?" Jacques asked doubtfully.

"In theory..." the dragon shifted awkwardly. In the form of a person, it looked weak and vulnerable and Jacques couldn't help but smile at it.

"Righto," she said decisively, and, using her arms to protect her face she closed her eyes and took a step forward.

She found herself in a dark murky corridor that smelt of damp air and bodily fluids. Suddenly the dragon was beside her.

"I can't believe that actually worked!" it said, examining their surroundings with trepidation.

"I'm not sure it did, completely," Jacques said, as she studied their surroundings intently. "How do we know this corridor is real?"

"It's not," the dragon said matter-of-factly. "This whole place is an illusion of collective consciousness."

"What does that mean? Lots of people built this place to hold magical prisoners?"

"Not exactly," the dragon began to explain. "On this plain, magic is much more powerful than on the one you came from. They people who were sent here believed that they were being imprisoned, so they created a prison for themselves."

"So you're saying their belief made it real? No, there must be more to it than that. After all, what's stopping them from starving to death? And if they imagined a prison, then surely they could imagine some sort of an escape route. Who in their right mind is going to sit here and rot?"

"There is more to it, but I don't know what yet. I will have a better understanding if I can find a person. If I can make contact I will be able to better ascertain the situation."

"I don't suppose you can say a word and make it light up in here? Evie can do that." With this last statement she was teasing the dragon.

"No," the dragon said, equally dryly. "Why don't you just use your sword?"

"My sword?" Jacques unsheathed the blade, which glowed brightly. "Wow, handier than a Swiss Army Knife, this," she observed, as she set forth through the darkness.

"The blade was cast for you and blessed. It will serve you in anyway required of it."

"Fantastic. Do you think it will do housework?"

The corridor seemed endless, but eventually they came to a door. It was massive and imposing and looked virtually impossible to break down.

"Do you think this is another illusion?" Jacques asked as she moved the glowing blade up and down the thick wooden barrier in the hope of illuminating a weakness to exploit.

"Everything here is an illusion."

"Alright then." Jacques shut her eyes and stepped forward through the door. When she opened them she found herself in a massive field. Birds were singing and in the background somewhere she could hear a stream trickling.

"Well, this is nice," she said to the dragon, who had appeared next to her. "All natury and stuff..."

"There!" The dragon pointed at a young girl sitting under a tree, seemingly asleep. Tentatively it walked over and lightly placed its hand on her shoulder. When it looked back up at Jacques its expression was that of concern. "They are stuck in circles in time: reliving the same traumatic moment over and over."

“You mean some sort of time loop? A moment from their past? How does that even work? What if nothing very traumatic ever happened?”

“Not from their past, from their future. Before they happen, we have an infinite number of possible futures ahead of us. The smallest decision can make an enormous change to our futures. Therefore, anyone has a possible traumatic event in their future, and this place seizes upon that traumatic moment to torture them.”

“Right. So, how do we snap them out of it?” Jacques asked, snapping her fingers repeatedly in the girl's face but to no avail.

“We need something from their reality to intrude upon their projected reality. If we can break the trance for one of them, the reality should be weakened for them all.”

“OK, so we should find Evie, I mean, we're from her reality, right? We should be able to snap her out of it?”

“Indeed.”

“Any ideas how we find her?”

“Do you have anything of hers? A personal possession? An object that she thinks is important? Something she cares about, perhaps?”

“I have nothing,” Jacques said despondently.

“That's alright...” the dragon said, looking at her with interest. “I know what to do.” It took her hand and closed its eyes.

Chapter Forty-One

"So, how do you plan to get her out?" Barry demanded as he examined the reams of appeal papers that Verm had scattered around him.

"I plan to appeal on the grounds of unsafe conviction, based on the fact that the person she is alleged to have murdered does not exist," Verm said firmly, handing Barry a pen. "You'll have to write it, I don't write your language."

"How d'you figure that?"

"The man she killed was an inquisitor from my world, there will be no record of him in this one."

"But she still killed him, it was self-defence, but she killed him, I don't see how his identity will change that."

"Well, it might not, but it will get her an appeal hearing, and that's when we make our move."

"Move?"

"I have something to get us back to my world. Once we are in court I'll get us out, you need to be waiting in your car. Once we're out we'll need to move quickly. Make sure you have what you need packed and ready to go. We won't be coming back here."

"All I need is her."

"Good. Get writing then – un-sou-nd-con-vic-tion..."

* * *

"I don't know what you're hoping to achieve by this," Karus said irritably, as she shifted in her seat attempting to pull her knee length skirt over her knees. "It doesn't make a difference who I killed, as far as they're concerned; I still killed someone, and showed no remorse. I feel none."

"Just be ready to follow my lead when the time comes," Verm said calmly as he adjusted his tie.

"All rise for the Right Honourable Judge Smithson," a clerk said loudly as the judge entered the room. As they rose to their feet a voice from behind them screamed:

"Time to die you murdering bitch!"

Verm turned sharply to see a woman holding a grenade.

"Is this your move? 'Cause it's really subtle," Karus said dryly, looking the woman up and down, searching for a weakness.

"No, but it'll do," Verm said calmly. Quick as a flash, he was over the barrier and snapped the woman's wrist as though it was nothing. Taking the grenade from her before she had time to pull the pin he tossed her to security who had already surrounded her. All focus was on the woman, who was screaming in pain, clutching her mutilated wrist. Verm looked to Karus, grabbed her arm and they hurried through the exit. It did not take security long to realise that they had taken advantage of the situation, and soon three men were in hot pursuit of them.

"Where is he?" Verm questioned the air in general, as he hurried to the bottom of the steps. At that moment Barry's tiny car screeched around the corner. The top was down and Verm literally picked Karus up and flung her into the back seat before leaping into the front next to Barry. "Drive!" he commanded.

"Hi, Honey!" Barry was beaming from ear to ear as they drove off at speed through the city streets, the sound of sirens gaining on them.

"I thought I told you not to involve him!" Karus was angry.

"I did what I must. He wouldn't help us unless he could be involved."

"And I suppose this is as far as your brilliant plan extends? We can't outrun police cars in this thing!"

"We don't need to outrun them for long," Verm informed her. "Just until we find a big enough wall."

"Careful what you wish for!" Barry screamed. They had turned down an alley which was a dead end. The wall of a massive red brick building was coming upon them at speed. Verm reached into his pocket and withdrew the bottle. He let them get as close to the wall as was possible before throwing it. They only had ten-seconds. Just as it looked like they were going to crash the portal appeared and they shot through the wall. “Hold your breath!”

When the flurry of rainbow and swirling sound subsided, they were in a dark forest and it was night.

“We made it,” Barry looked around in disbelief.

“Do you have what we need?” Verm asked.

“In here.” Barry opened the dashboard to reveal a polished walnut box.

“This will do it?” Verm asked, taking the box and unclipping the brass clasp to reveal a syringe of clear liquid nestled in blue velvet protective padding.

“That is one hundred percent synthetic poison. It'll do it.”

“Excellent.” Verm shut the box and returned it to Barry, who put it in his backpack.

Barry turned to face Karus. “Hi,” he grinned.

“Hi.” She smiled back. They kissed.

Verm climbed out over the door of the car, which was jammed by some bushes. He looked around and listened to the air.

“What is it?” Barry began, but Verm raised his arm to silence him.

“There's a fire, over there. It must be people, keep it down.” But it was too late, there was a sound of cracking twigs as someone was moving towards them to investigate the noise.

“Weapons!” Verm hissed urgently.

Barry pulled the keys from the ignition and scrambled to open the boot, which was where Verm's weapons were stored. The footsteps were becoming closer. Karus leapt over the bonnet. Her power was the same as Yfrey's, the ability to channel the elements. However, Karus had had ten years to practise channelling her power in a world where magic did not flourish easily. As such, now that she had returned to her world, her power was increased tenfold. The wind seemed to carry her over the trees to the sound of the approaching footsteps. She came upon a dark haired man approaching them, sword drawn. She forced forward her hand, channelling through it the power of the wind. A loud boom accompanied the movement, as the speed of the gust she sent powering towards the man smashed the sound barrier. He flew backwards and landed on his rear, with the wind knocked out of him. Gasping for air he looked up to see his assailant.

"Hi Aunt Karus!" he coughed.

"Torius," she lowered herself to the ground and looked at him. "What have you done to yourself?"

"What was necessary," he said defensively, struggling to his feet.

"It's funny what terrified people deem necessary," Karus mused, offering him her hand. "Fear is a strange motivator."

"I am not afraid. I did what I must to protect Yfrey. You abandoned us!"

"Look at you. You're a terrified little boy shouting about things he doesn't understand. What are you doing here?"

"I'm looking for Yfrey."

"She isn't here."

"No kidding."

"I mean she is not in this world. I would be able to sense her."

"But you couldn't sense me?"

"You have contaminated your essence with dark magic. There is nothing left of you."

At that point Verm and Barry arrived. Verm had a sword and Barry was wielding a handgun.

"Oh, it's you," Verm lowered his weapon.

"Nice to see you too, Big Guy," Torius said ironically.

"Where's the tracker?"

"He was useless, so I let him go."

"You killed him."

"No, I let him go. I'm not a complete monster."

"Whatever you say."

"Yfrey isn't in this world," Karus repeated for the newcomers.

"Then we should get to my father's cottage. He and his seer could be in danger. I would never have left, but they said it was important."

"We aren't far from there, come on." Torius was relieved to break from his aunt's judging gaze.

As they arrived on the outskirts of the cottage they could see soldiers surrounding the entrance. Borana and Portan were on their knees at the feet of an inquisitor.

"Can you create a distraction?" Verm asked Karus in a harsh whisper.
"Of course I can," she smiled. "I like being on the same team as you, Verm. Fighting always seemed wrong."
With that, she allowed the wind to pick her up and carry her over the men. Storm clouds rushed in from all directions, and rather than Yfrey's preferred weapon of lightning, Karus chose hail stones the size of rocks to bombard the soldiers with. In the panic and confusion, they scattered, but did not make it beyond the blades of Verm and Torius. The inquisitor looked up and saw Karus looming. Laughing he picked up a rifle from the floor where one of the fleeing soldiers dropped it.
"Foolish witch!" He pointed the rifle at she soared above him. "You cannot frighten me with your parlour tricks."
The click of the hammer of a gun behind his ear made him falter.
"Drop it..." Barry's voice trembled. The inquisitor turned slowly to face his assailant. Barry's hand was shaking as he held the gun. The inquisitor smiled wryly.
"You are not a part of this, are you? Just put down the gun and walk away."
"You put yours down," Barry did not sound convincing. "You think I won't use this, but I will."
"No, you won't," Karus had alighted softly on the ground and was standing next to the inquisitor. "You are not a killer and you won't become one for me."
"He won't have to." With all the focus on Barry no-one had noticed Portan rise from his knees and take up another discarded rifle. He did not offer the inquisitor an ultimatum, or wait to see if he would relinquish his weapon. He simply pulled the trigger and sent his brains splattering to the ground.
Barry did not lower his gun hand. Still trembling the weapon was now pointed at his wife.
"Barry," she spoke softly. "It's over, you can put it down."
"Is he..."

“He's dead. You can put the gun down now, it's alright.” Shakily, he let her take the gun from his trembling hand. She handed it to Portan and threw her arms around Barry in a tight embrace.

“That's why I didn't want you here,” she whispered to him. “You are too gentle for this place. Gentle people become hard or die. I don't want either to happen to you.” She looked at him sadly.

“I lost you once, I won't lose you again. I'm your husband, I should be able to protect you.”

“Here!” Torius interrupted them. “How did they find you? Calim should be on the run by now.”

“Perhaps if you hadn't killed every one of them you could have asked...” Borana suggested.

“You killed all of them?” Karus looked at Verm in utter disbelief. “What the hell kind of strategist are you?”

“They knew you'd come for me,” Portan said calmly. “This was a distraction.”

Chapter Forty-Two

It was the most strange sensation – Jacques felt her whole body dissolve as the dragon touched her, and as it reformed they were in some sort of barn. Yfrey was curled up in the corner, in the foetal position, tears streaming down her cheeks, though she was clearly unconscious.

"What do we do now?" There was audible concern in Jacques' voice.

"Wake her up," the dragon spoke calmly.

Jacques knelt down beside Yfrey, placed one hand on her shoulder and the other gently over her clenched hands. She spoke quietly to her.

"Evie, you need to wake up now."

Yfrey held the lifeless body in her arms, rocking back and forth. She could not do anything else. If she let go, then everything would be over. She could see buildings burning in the background and bodies being carried away on wooden boards, but she could not hear anything. It was as though all the pain and violence that surrounded her was engulfed in a great bubble which absorbed all sounds that entered it. Suddenly, clearly through the silence, she heard a familiar voice.

"Evie, you need to wake up now."

"Jacques?" she loosened her grip on the body and looked down to see if it was speaking to her. It was still in her arms.

"Evie, wake up. It's time to go!" the voice spoke again. Suddenly it was as though the world were travelling at infinite speed, taking her breath with it. As she struggled to breathe, the whole world seemed to disintegrate around her and she found herself curled up on the floor with Jacques looking down at her.

"Hey, welcome back," she smiled gently at her.

"Jacques!" Yfrey leapt up and threw her arms around her. "You died and it was all my fault!"

"Well, that didn't happen yet," Jacques said, awkwardly returning the hug. "And if we work out how it did happen then we can prevent it. It was only one possible future."

After Yfrey had relayed the events of her imprisonment, she looked to Jacques for answers.

"Your brother is a complete moron."

"Well, he wasn't always, he became very angry after our parents died."

"I don't want to argue about him. I don't even want to think about him. It's simple anyway. We aim for a capture instead of a kill, problem solved."

"Yfrey," the dragon spoke quietly to her. "Can you break through this false reality?"

For the first time Yfrey looked around her. Nothing was real. She held the stone that still hung around her neck tightly in order to channel her power through it.

"Nochtann!" She spoke loudly and clearly and their surroundings evaporated. Suddenly they were out in the open, many confused people were all around. Some were extremely emaciated, and amongst the people, lying on the ground were dead bodies.

"Dammit! We should have come sooner!" Jacques managed to disguise the tears that she was choking back behind anger.

"There is no way we could have known about this," Yfrey spoke firmly. "As soon as Calim took them they were under a death sentence. We have saved a lot."

"And what are we supposed to do with them now?" Jacques demanded. "They certainly aren't in any state to fight and won't survive where we need to be."

"I'll take them back with me," the dragon spoke calmly. "We can nurse them back to health on the island. You can return for them when you are done."

"It could be a while."

"I understand."

The dragon transformed into a dragon three times the size of the one that Jacques rescued from the hunters. The throngs of people looked at it in awe, but they were not afraid. Yfrey turned to speak to them.

"Jacques and I have to return to our reality. Calim is on the run, and we need to finish what we have begun. The dragon will take care of you all, go with it, you'll be safe."

One by one the people climbed onto the back of the giant dragon. An old woman stopped next to Jacques and handed her a vile of liquid.

"This one," she spoke shakily "will take you where you need to be." She closed Jacques' hand around the bottle and looked at her.

"Er... thanks..." Jacques wrenched her hand away and put the vial into her trouser pocket. The old woman walked slowly towards the dragon.

"Well, that wasn't a bit creepy, at all," Jacques said to Yfrey, as the dragon took off. "Hope I don't need to be anywhere that badly. So, what do you reckon, can you get us back?"

"We can try my stick."

"Sure, go for it. What's wrong?"

"What if my stick doesn't work in my world?"

"One way to find out." A portal appeared in front of them. "Nice work."

"I didn't do it."

"Guess they need us... how do we know this will take us where we need to go?" Jacques asked uncertainly as she poked the portal with the tip of her sword.

"We don't, we'll have to take it on faith."

"It just seems awfully convenient that this portal should appear just as we need it."

"Well, we have to assume that since we disappeared they've been trying to get us back. And Borana is a seer, so she would know when and where to place a portal."

"I don't know; it just seems a bit too easy..." Jacques prodded it again.

"Well, what do you suggest?" Yfrey asked. "I don't know another way of getting back, do you?"

"I kinda thought I was the muscle in this relationship," Jacques retorted dryly. "You're the one who does all the thinking."

"Well, hold your breath then." Yfrey took Jacques by the hand and together they leapt through the portal.

They landed squarely in the middle of Verm's command tent, which was empty.

“This is where we needed to be?” Jacques asked dubiously.

Suddenly there was a cry from outside of “We're under attack! Man the barricades!”

“Apparently so!” Yfrey reached into her belt for her dagger. “Still a stick,” she said frustratedly.

“How many times? It's a wand! Ah, forget it!” Jacques drew her sword and flew out of the tent.

“Roghnaithe!” One of the soldiers spoke respectfully as he saw her. “When did you arrive?”

“Just now. I only travel by portal these days. Where's the attack?”

“Follow me?”

The barricades on the north-east side of the stronghold were down and an army of men were piling through. The men who had been defending the wall were labourers and working men, and were not trained for war. Without Verm to direct them they were sitting ducks.

“Regroup!” Jacques screamed as she approached. “Fall back and regroup!”

The men looked blankly at her and the onslaught of enemy soldiers took advantage of the situation and started cutting them down.

“Where the hell is Vern when you need him?” Jacques demanded as she leapt into the fray. She was agile and her martial arts training combined with her skill with a blade soon told the onslaught of soldiers that they weren't just dealing with shop keepers and land workers any more. They backed off and formed a circle around her. She stood defensively in the centre, her eyes darting around the men to see which one of them planned to move first. She was vastly outnumbered and she knew it.

As her eyes darted from soldier to soldier she suddenly became aware that none of them were moving. Not a shiver or an involuntary twitch.

Tentatively, Yfrey stepped through the circle holding her wand.

“Quite useful this stick,” she observed as she made her way to Jacques.

“What did you do?”

“I don't really know. I wanted them to stop attacking you, and they did. I don't know how long it will last.”

"Right! You men!" Jacques called to the rebels who were still standing. "Disarm them, and when they can move again tell them they've lost and if they surrender no harm will come to them."

"Where are you going?" Yfrey asked.

"To find Calim and finish this."

"I'll come with you."

"No, help these men secure the barricades."

"Be careful."

"Always am." Jacques gave Yfrey's hand a reassuring squeeze and raced off over the wall. She knew Calim would be hanging back, he was a coward.

Chapter Forty-Three

"This isn't right," Borana said urgently. "We were supposed to die. They wanted to distract you from your goal, but in my vision it didn't work. We died but you won the city. I don't know what's supposed to happen now, it isn't right."

"Something must have affected the time-line." Karus said calmly. "I think it is for the better that you survived."

"What are we compared to all those men trying to hold the barricade," Borana objected. "It isn't right."

"You are important," Verm spoke seriously to her, putting his hand gently on her arm. "We saved you for a purpose. Where we came through, it would have been at least three days from Central City, and our vehicle is unusable. Now you can conjure a portal, we'll be there in no time. You're important. We lost nothing by saving you and gained everything. You are important."

Borana looked at the huge man who stood before her. He had seemed so terrifying in the tavern, now there was something kind and gentle about him.

"I'll get to work on the portal."

"Thank you."

"Why, Verm, I didn't know you had it in you."

"You constantly underestimated me," Verm smiled a little sadly at Karus.

"You underestimated me too," she indicated his scar.

"I would have let you go, you know."

"What?"

"So, what's the plan?" Barry hurried into the living room where the two of them were talking.

"The plan is you stay here," Verm said firmly. "You are not prepared for where we're going."

“Give the box to me,” Karus held out her hand. Barry smiled sadly and took the box with the syringe from his pack and handed it to her.
“What's that?” Torius demanded, cracking his neck as he walked into the room.
“Synthetic poison,” Barry informed him.
“For Calim?”
“Yes.”
“Give it to me,” he held out his hand. “I'll keep it safe in my pack.”
Karus handed him the box, which he tucked into the pack that hung from his waist.
“You will be careful?” Barry spoke quietly to his wife.
“Of course. I'll come back for you, don't worry.”
“I always worry about you.”
“I know,” she kissed him.
“It's ready.” Borana entered the room again. “As you approach the gnarled tree by the far moss rock, it will appear. It will disappear again after five minutes, so you'll need to go straight through.”
“Thank you,” Verm smiled at her.
Karus returned Barry's gun to him. “Take care of yourself, I'll be back as soon as I can.”
He laid it down gently on the arm of the chair and watched them leave.
“Come on, Son,” Portan placed a comforting hand on his shoulder. “I'll teach you a game.”

* * *

Their portal emerged on the outskirts of Central City. From the safety of the wooded area where Yfrey and Verm had first met the young boy, they could see that the barricade was under attack.
“Yfrey is here,” Karus looked up sharply. “I can sense her.”
“Find her,” Verm commanded. “We'll defend the barricade.” He slapped Torius on the upper arm to demonstrate camaraderie, and the two men hurried off to join the fray.
Jacques was on the outskirts of the barricade, battling enemy soldiers. It seemed that there were more who were loyal to Calim than could have been

anticipated. Of course, he could not have achieved such a position of power through fear alone. He was charismatic and had his followers convinced that the threat posed by the magical people was far greater than anything that could be inflicted on them by him. As such they fought for their very existence, and desperate men could be vicious and frightening. She was knocked to the ground and her sword flew from her hand. A man holding a mace loomed over her. She covered her face with her hand waiting for the death blow, but it never came. As she looked up Torius was standing over her.

"Hi there," he offered her his hand.

"You took your time," she allowed him to help her up.

"Catch up later!" Verm called, lifting her sword with his foot and sending it through the air towards her. She leapt in the air and caught it by the handle, as she landed, she prevented a blow from landing on Torius.

"We're even."

"Whatever."

Between the three of them, they swiftly dispatched the attack on the barricade and those men who were not injured, retreated.

"Where's Calim?" Jacques demanded of one who was lying on the ground, injured.

"You'll get nothing from me," he spat at her.

"I'll get it out of him!" Torius pulled her out of the way and knelt menacingly beside the man.

"No!" Jacques pulled him away by the shoulder and sent him sprawling in the mud. "I will not resort to torture, I will find another way." She turned to Verm, who was talking to the men on the other side of the barricade. With the help of Yfrey and Karus they had quelled the onslaught and were rebuilding the barricade and helping to get the wounded to the medical facility Verm had instituted. "Get these men medical attention," she instructed him. "Set up a prison ward if you have to, but don't leave them here, we're better than this."

Verm nodded. "Medics!" he bellowed over the barricade and four men came running. "Get all the injured medical attention, not just our side. Keep them guarded but make them comfortable."

"You're a good man, Vern," she smiled at him.

As he was being carried away, one of the fallen men grabbed her arm and looked at her.

"Calim is just over the north west ridge, he has a seer with him, he'll know you're coming."

"Aw, you mean it won't be a surprise? Gosh darn it!" Jacques pushed her hair out of her face, which was stained with blood and mud. She looked terrifying. "It's time to end this." She spoke determinedly.

"I'm going with you," Verm said, matching her stride.

"No, you need to stay with Evie. She won't cope if neither of us come back."

"I don't know about you, but I'm planning on coming back," Verm said frankly.

"Vern, please. You're needed here."

"Victory and honour Roghnaithe." Verm stood up straight and saluted her.

"Victory and Honour, Vern." She smiled weakly and strode out over the ridge to meet Calim.

Chapter Forty-Four

"What do you mean, you see nothing?" Calim demanded angrily, kicking the seer in the stomach.

"I'm sorry, My Lord," the man coughed from the ground. "I don't see anything."

"That's because it's over." Jacques entered the clearing, sword drawn. "You'll want to leave, now." She spoke to the seer without taking her eyes off of Calim. The seer scuttled away.

"Coward!" Calim spat on the floor.

"I guess you just don't inspire loyalty." Jacques said flatly.

"So, you've come to kill me. Do you really think you can?" Calim asked mockingly.

"No, I've come to take you into custody. How easy that is, is up to you."

"It's not going to be easy," Calim drew his sword.

"I was hoping you'd say that." Jacques charged him.

They battled fiercely until Jacques managed to flick Calim's sword from his hand. Catching the sword in her free hand, she crossed the blades and brought them up to his throat.

"Yield," she said firmly.

"Alright, Roghnaithe, you win." Calim raised his hands to show surrender. Jacques watched him carefully, but did not see the concealed blade up his sleeve. As he raised his hands to show submission he slashed her upper arm deeply. She cried out in pain and dropped one sword. Just as quickly with the other hand she turned her blade on its size and smashed him about the temple, knocking him to the floor unconscious.

As he fell, she too she fell to her knees, dropping her blade and looking at her arm. It was bleeding hard. She tried to take her jacket off to examine the damage, but was unable to move it. She looked around desperately. What could she do now? Calim wouldn't be unconscious for long, and she couldn't stay here anyway. It was likely that before long she would lose too much blood and pass out.

She looked around, not sure what she was looking for. Then she heard footsteps behind her. Picking up her sword with her good arm she turned shakily on her knees.

"Who's there?" she demanded.

"Jacques?" it was a voice she recognised, but had not heard in a long time.

"Carys?"

"Hi," Karus knelt down to be eye level with her.

"What are you doing here?"

"Looking for you. Let's sort your arm out, we need to stop that bleeding until we can get you to a medic."

Karus removed her suit jacket and ripped both sleeves from her pin striped blouse. Tightly she bound the wound, one sleeve over the other to stop the bleeding.

"Come on, that's not very good, we need to get you to a medic," she said firmly.

"We need to bring him," Jacques indicated the unconscious Calim. "Check his sleeves for weapons."

"Right," Karus unstrapped the blade from his wrist before kicking off her shoes and removing her tights. Then she replaced her shoes. "At least these ridiculous clothes are good for something." She used the tights to hog tie Calim and, taking the central knot in both hands, she proceeded to walk backward, dragging the unconscious Calim through the mud.

"Well, I was going to say that you looked very smart, until you ripped off your sleeves and used your tights for bondage." Jacques carried one sword and wore the other in her belt.

"I was in court today," Karus informed her.

"How'd that work out for you?"

"It was a blast."

"Nice."

"Yeah."

"So, how have you been?"

"You know, staying in a lot, took up smoking for a while."

"That shit'll kill you."

"So they tell me. How about you?"

"Oh, you know, fighting an evil dictator, saving an oppressed people, the usual."

"Sounds exciting."

"Well, Crazy Thrill Ride is my middle name."

"I thought it was Murial?"

"And you never tell anyone that."

"Cross my heart."

"Vern!" Jacques could see the mighty figure of Verm standing on top of the barricade, directing men. Upon hearing her voice, he turned, leapt down and ran to meet them.

"You did it!" he exclaimed, taking Calim from Karus and throwing him over his shoulder as though he was nothing.

"He'll need medical attention," Jacques said weakly. She was feeling tired.

"So do you," Verm observed with concern, looking at her arm. The blood had seeped through both bandages and was bright red.

"I'm OK."

"Stop being a hero," Karus commanded. "You've done your job, now let us help you." She put her arm around Jacques' waist to help support her. Jacques was too tired to argue and allowed herself to be supported. As they entered the hospital building, they were met by Yfrey.

"Evie! What are you doing here? Are you hurt?"

"No, I'm fine, but Torius was. Nothing serious but he needed patching up. And he helped me carry some other people here. But you are!" Seeing Jacques' arm she rushed to her.

"I'm fine! Fuss over nothing!" As she spoke Jacques' knees buckled and Yfrey rushed to support her from the other side.

"Find her a doctor!" Verm spoke authoritatively. "I'll find a private room for this." He dumped Calim on the floor as though he was sick of carrying him. He grunted as though he was beginning to stir, but did not move.

"You did it!" Yfrey smiled broadly at Jacques.

"Told you I would."

"I know."

Chapter Forty-Five

"How are you feeling?" Verm asked as he came quietly into the hospital room, holding what looked like the branch of a tree.

"I'm much better, thank you." Jacques smiled. It had been three days and she had wanted to leave much sooner, but the doctor had wanted to observe her. Yfrey was asleep in the chair. She had taken it upon herself to stand guard, for fear Jacques would flee. "What's with the branch?"

"Karus tells me that it is traditional in your society to bring a plant when visiting someone in hospital."

"Well, yes... It's very nice, thank you. You can put it over there."

Obediently Verm placed the branch on the table.

"How's everything going? Yfrey won't tell me anything, afraid stress will slow my recovery."

"Things are going well, we are taking down the barricades. Since you brought in Calim, there have been no more attacks. We are just trying to rebuild the city, then it may be time to attempt to form some sort of government – I don't know how to do that."

"Best thing would be to hold an election, I guess." Jacques said thoughtfully. "You should probably be in charge until everything is rebuilt. Then ask people if they want to run for government, maybe you could work with a team of civilians in the meantime so a group of you are doing it. There mustn't be one person with too much power."

"You are very wise."

"It's probably the blood loss. Is Calim secure?"

“Yes, he is locked in a room up the hall. There are two guards with him at all times. I don't know what we are going to do with him, though. We can't keep him here indefinitely.”

“Well, when he has no more sway over people we can let him go. Until then just have to keep him locked somewhere.”

“Perhaps we should build a prison.”

“It's a thought.”

“Alright. Well, I'm glad you're feeling better. I'm going back to my command tent. When you're up to it, or Yfrey allows, maybe you could come and join me? I'd appreciate your input on some things.”

“Thanks, Vern. Hey, before you go, could you pass me my trousers from that chair? I think I'll go stretch my legs.”

Verm handed her the trousers and walked quietly out.

* * *

“Can you let me in? I want to talk to him.” Torius spoke to the guards outside Calim's room.

“The general said no-one was to go in or out, Sir,” the guard said respectfully.

“Well, he didn't mean me, ask him, I'll wait.”

The guard looked at his partner uncertainly, who nodded at him.

“How are you, Brean?” Torius asked the remaining guard.

“Very well, T. We knew we'd win in the end though, eh? Was all worth it. How pathetic, in there now? Has to ask my permission when he wants to piss!”

“We won. Your mate won't find Verm, he's gone back to his command tent. Just give me five minutes, it'll be OK.”

“Alright, five minutes, but don't rough him up or anything, I'll get the blame.”

“Don't worry.”

Torius entered the room. Calim was tied to the bed.

“Torius,” he looked up weakly. He was broken. “Come to taunt me?”

“No, I've come to kill you.” Torius took the wooden box from his pouch.

* * *

Jacques stared out of the window overlooking the city. It was mostly rubble. There were people clearing, others building, some were just milling around. They all seemed relaxed, as though a huge weight had been lifted. She smiled.

"Ma'am? Ma'am!" Jacques turned, realising the man was talking to her.

"What is it?"

"The general, have you seen the general?"

"He went back to his command tent. Why? What's the matter?"

"Mr. Torius, Ma'am. He said the general wouldn't mind him going in to see the prisoner, said I could check with the general."

"I'm certain that the general would mind. Tell him he can't," Jacques said firmly. Torius was not even here and he was annoying her.

"He's a very difficult man to say no to," the guard began awkwardly.

"Alright, take me to him."

As they approached the door, they saw one man standing outside.

"Maybe he left?" the guard offered hopefully.

"He didn't leave," Jacques said irritably. "You let him in, didn't you?" she addressed Brean.

"He said he only needed five minutes..."

"Yes, he's very persuasive." She pushed past the guard and into the room. Calim was on the bed, dead. The wooden box was open on the table with the empty syringe lying on top of it. Torius was sitting in the chair by the bed, his skin was grey.

"What did you do?" she demanded.

"What I had to. What you couldn't."

"You've killed yourself!"

"You won't cry for me."

"No, but Evie will. You are evil and selfish..." her voice broke.

"Well, it's a good thing I'm dead," he gasped and died.

"You idiot!" Jacques punched Torius' body in frustration.

"Jacques?" Yfrey called from down the corridor.

"Evie, no..." Jacques hurried out of the room.

"Jacques! Where have you been? You're supposed to be resting. What were you doing in there?"

"Evie, don't..." but Yfrey had already pushed past her into the room.

“You promised you wouldn't!”

“I didn't! I promise, Evie. You have to believe me, I didn't do it.”

“No-one else could have!”

“Torius did it! He injected Calim with something! It wasn't me, Evie, I promise!”

“Why would he do that?” Tears were starting to roll down Yfrey's cheeks as she collapsed to her knees.

“He was very angry,” Jacques knelt down beside her. “I don't think he wanted to live if he had no-one to fight.”

“I could have helped him, I should have tried.”

“There is nothing you could have done.” Jacques flopped down from a kneeling position to putting all her weight on the side of her leg. She felt a crack in her pocket like glass breaking. “What the...” she went to stand up, but realised that there was no ground beneath her. It was like she was falling, but didn't know where. Everything was dark.

“Jacques?” Yfrey looked around desperately. “Jacques?”

“What happened?” the guards rushed in.

“I don't know, it's like something engulfed her.”

“Are they dead?”

“Yes.” Yfrey was suddenly reminded of the two corpses in the room with her. “Verm can deal with that, there's nothing I can do. I need to speak to my aunt, I have to find Jacques.” She hurried out.

Epilogue

Jacques opened her eyes to see blue flashing lights. It seemed to be night and she could hear sirens. There was a voice above her head.

"She's opening her eyes. Miss, Miss? Can you hear me?"

"What's going on? Where am I?"

"You're on Queen's Road. Can you tell me how you got here?"

"Queen's Road?"

"Yes, Queen's Road. You seem to have suffered some serious injuries over a period of time. Do you know what happened?"

"I was in a war. It was another world. Am I home now?"

"Yeah, you're home now. We are going to take you to Red Hill General to get you checked out. I'm going to give you something to relax you."

"Red Hill General? That's where I was born. Am I really home?"

"Yes ma'am. You're home. You're safe now. Just relax."

"What do you reckon? War vet? PTSD?" one paramedic said to the other.

"Maybe, but that doesn't explain these injuries, she was tortured. We'll know more when the doc checks her out – but I'd say she was kidnapped, possibly for months. No ID on her?"

"Nothing."

"Well, let's get her to Red Hill, they'll find out more then."

About The Author

With a background in community and music journalism, as well as bra fitting (which she never wishes to speak of) C H Clepitt is the author of a number of books and short stories. Clepitt is currently the badger in charge of satirical news website Newsnibbles.co.uk as well as a number of other projects. Find out more and sign up for the newsletter at chclepitt.com.

Follow and say hello to C H Clepitt on Twitter @BadgersTweetToo and Facebook @CHClepitt – she'd probably like the company.

If you enjoyed this book, then please support the author by leaving a review.

Also by C H Clepitt

A Reason to Stay

Who would have thought that being knocked out by a plus sized mannequin would lead to a complete life change?
Stephen is stuck in a rut: dead-end job, no romantic prospects, no hope. A series of bizarre accidents look set to change his path forever.
Having been given a year off work, Stephen decides to undertake a journey across country, aboard a less than manly, nonetheless affordable mode of transportation. A near miss with a miniature poodle leaves Stephen in a cast, his moped wrecked and his journey postponed; he is forced to spend 6 weeks in a village.

His physical journey at a standstill, trapped amongst a quirky cast of characters, Stephen finds himself on a different kind of journey, that of self

discovery. Learning more about these people makes him discover new things about himself, and gradually his angry, sarcastic world view dissipates. Life in the village seems perfect, but surely this idyllic existence can't last, especially for someone as hopelessly accident prone as Stephen?
A Reason to Stay playfully satirises society. Follow Stephen's adventures whilst he conquers his fear of shopping, teenagers and lascivious older women, in a humorous yet strangely real tale of the effect one person can have on those around them without even realising.

I Wore Heels To The Apocalypse

Is anyone truly prepared for the apocalypse? Well, Kerry certainly isn't, and she fairly quickly discovers that looking sharp in a business suit and heels is not going to help anyone when there's an apocalypse, with possible zombies!

Together with a super spy, an ex girl guide and a personal trainer with manly foraging skills Kerry must battle terrifying religious cults, rich people and her personal demons, all whilst having the daily chore of deciding what to wear!

This is a laugh out loud comedy with romance, heart and talking badgers, and is not to be missed.

What would you wear to the apocalypse? #IWoreHeels

Lightning Source UK Ltd.
Milton Keynes UK
UKHW011025111019
351418UK00006B/88/P